"Dangerous?" Margu_____ Say-
brook dangerous? He see_____ _as, in fact,
manners far more agreeab_____ ___ Sir Richard!"

"Of course he does, Miss _____ ne snapped. "I am no
womanizer! And he uses th___ _harming manners to advantage. He is not to be trusted with any young woman, particularly one so innocent of the world as your sister!"

"And yet Lady Norwood is a good friend of a man with
such a reprehensible reputation?" she demanded. "Surely she
would not allow such a man into her intimate circle of friends."

Sir Richard laughed. "I see that you still do not know my
stepmother well, Miss Standish. So long as he pays court to
her, any man is welcome in her 'intimate circle.' You would
do well to remember that. And you would do well to keep
your sister away from that circle."

"I note, Sir Richard, that you do not say that I would do
well to keep myself away," she observed dryly. "Is there a
particular reason for that?"

He gave her a short bow. "But of course, Miss Standish. I
have seen from the first that you are formed of a different
metal from your sister. I have no doubt that you will handle
yourself very well in any situation. You are, after all, my stepmother's namesake. Why should I expect your behavior to be
any different from hers?"

And so saying he transferred the ribbons to his left hand,
reached down and, with his right arm, caught her to him and
kissed her firmly. "And if you persist in driving out alone with
a man, Miss Standish, you might as well know the kind of
behavior you may expect. Consider this a lesson . . ."

Books by Mona Gedney

A LADY OF FORTUNE
THE EASTER CHARADE
A VALENTINE'S DAY GAMBIT
A CHRISTMAS BETROTHAL
A SCANDALOUS CHARADE
A DANGEROUS AFFAIR

Published by Zebra Books

A
Dangerous
Affair

Mona Gedney

ZEBRA BOOKS
KENSINGTON PUBLISHING CORP.

One

The spring storm gusted through the garden surrounding the ancient brick house and slapped rain derisively against its windows. In the library a fire glowed bravely, doing its best to soften the threadbare furnishings and surrendering only occasionally to the storm with a sooty billow of smoke. Marguerite sighed. Glancing around the room, its wood floors and paneling as polished as she could make them, the old desk and the tea table shining in the firelight, its fitful gleam softening the scratches that years of service had inflicted upon them, she felt as though she had much in common with that fire. The bookshelves that lined the room were empty now, the volumes all neatly packed away. The tapestry draperies, faded to a dull yellow, were too worn to withstand the sudden blasts of cold, and she drew her shawl more closely about her shoulders, thinking that there was nothing quite as bone-chilling as the death throes of winter. She and the fire had done their best to make the old room cheerful, but they were fighting a losing battle. However, she, like the fire, surrendered only occasionally.

Another crack of thunder ripped through the night, and the two young women in the library responded to the fury outside in a manner typical of each. Marguerite, a diminutive brunette, continued her sewing with an air of cheerful determination, while her sister, a slender, silver-haired girl, started up from her book with every clap of thunder and finally closed it, giving up any pretense of reading.

Before she could speak, a pounding at the front door rose above the noise of the storm. At that unexpected sound, both young ladies rose and stared at each other.

"Who would come to see us in such a storm as this?" asked Celia nervously.

"And at such a late hour?" responded her sister, laying down her sewing. "Well, I had best go and see before they drown. It is a thousand pities that we had to let Mrs. Dillard go. She would have made short work of any uninvited callers."

Having someone call upon them at such an hour was most unusual, for the people of the village knew that their housekeeper had gone and that they now lived alone. Only an emergency was likely to bring someone to their door at this late hour. Marguerite was not nervous, however. They had lived in the old rectory at the foot of the village all of their lives with never a hint of trouble.

As she opened the door, another sudden gust of wind sent a cold spray of rain across her face, and the man standing there stepped quickly into the entry.

"Forgive me for troubling you, Miss Standish," he said smoothly, removing his hat. "And for causing such a mess," he added, seeing the rivulets of water descend from his greatcoat onto the polished wood of the floor.

"Have you had an accident, Mr. Beezley?" inquired Marguerite coolly.

He looked startled by her question, his pale eyes glinting in the candlelight. "An accident?" he asked. "Why should you think that?"

"It is very late, Mr. Beezley," she pointed out patiently. "And you know that my sister and I live here alone now, so it is scarcely proper to call upon us at this hour unless there is some pressing matter that brings you."

"That is it!" he replied eagerly, seizing upon her words.

"I must speak to you now, Miss Standish! I could not let any more time go by."

She looked at him with distaste. Of all her father's parishioners, Vincent Beezley was her least favorite. He was well-looking enough and he possessed a comfortable income, but he had also buried two wives in quick succession, each of them having given birth to three children, and those six children were the terrors of the neighborhood. It was rumored, too, that his wives had been little more than household chattels and had died to escape him and the children. Marguerite, having watched Beezley and the children, believed the rumors.

"You could not allow any more time to go by before what, Mr. Beezley?" she asked unencouragingly, certain now of the nature of his errand.

"Couldn't we go in by the fire to talk, Miss Standish?" he returned, glancing toward the lighted door of the library.

"Not at this hour, sir. I believe that it would be better if you were brief. As I said, since Celia and I are here alone—"

"And that is it exactly!" he interrupted her. "You and your sister *are* alone, and something must be done about it!"

She stared at him, her eyebrows lifted. She knew what was coming next, but she could see no way to stop him.

"When I was at the Green Dragon tonight, I heard it said that you might be leaving soon for London. I determined then that I must come and speak to you immediately. I could not wait until tomorrow and risk losing Miss Celia!"

Marguerite's expression grew colder, but Mr. Beezley, oblivious to anything save the sound of his own voice, talked on. "I think that you must allow me to speak to Miss Celia now, and to make her my offer before you take her away to the ruinous life of London. She is too delicate to live in such a place."

Marguerite, thinking of his two wives in the churchyard,

replied dryly, "Some find the climate here dangerous for their health, Mr. Beezley. And there is no point in continuing this conversation, for we have spoken of this before."

She had been horrified the first time that he had talked of marrying Celia. It had been immediately after their father's accident, and she had told him that it was much too soon after the funeral to think of such matters. He had waited for six weeks and tried again, but she had firmly rebuffed him once more, saying that Celia, at seventeen, was too young to be thinking of marriage. She had not added that she would consider her sister too young for marriage at thirty if the man offering were Vincent Beezley.

"And I told you on both occasions, Miss Standish, that your father had agreed that I would be allowed to offer for her as soon as she passed her seventeenth birthday. That happy event occurred last month."

"And I am not my father, Mr. Beezley. I shall not allow you to pay your addresses to her now or a year from now."

Beezley took a step closer to her. He was a tall man, and he towered above Marguerite. "You are no more than a girl yourself, Miss Standish," he said, his voice rougher now. "Perhaps you are jealous of your sister's opportunity."

Before he could continue, there was a sharp rapping at the door and Marguerite slipped around him, grateful for the interruption. She was not afraid of the likes of Vincent Beezley, but she was not anxious for what promised to be an ugly scene.

"Why, Mr. Clive, what a pleasant surprise!" she exclaimed, opening the door wide for him. "Do come in out of the storm."

Mr. Clive, the young man who had come to take her father's place as rector, looked from her face to that of Vincent Beezley and said slowly, "I was out for my evening constitutional when I saw the carriage in front of your home. I feared that there was a problem here and I wanted to see if I could be of any help."

Beezley snorted in disbelief. "Out for a walk in weather such as this?" he exclaimed. "Only a fool would be out tonight!"

"But you are here, too, are you not, Mr. Beezley?" inquired the young rector gently, drying his spectacles carefully on his handkerchief.

Beezley flushed and took a step toward him, but remembered himself in time and stopped. Even a young and foolish man of the cloth was worthy of some respect. "I will speak to you at a more convenient time, Miss Standish," he said stiffly, placing his hat firmly on his head.

"There will be no convenient time, Mr. Beezley," she assured him as he turned away. "You have my answer now, and it will not change."

His only reply was the slamming of the door behind him.

"A remarkably boorish man," remarked Mr. Clive, staring after him thoughtfully. "Although I should not say that of my parishioners, I suppose. Are you all right, Miss Standish?"

Marguerite smiled gratefully. "Thanks to you, Mr. Clive, we are now doing very nicely. Mr. Beezley was impolitely demanding that I allow him to offer for my sister."

Mr. Clive nodded grimly. "I thought as much. I was taking my supper late at the Green Dragon, and I heard his reaction when someone mentioned that they supposed that you and Miss Celia would be leaving for London soon. I was afraid that he might do something ill-considered such as this when he left in so great a hurry."

"And we are very grateful that you came out into the rain on our behalf, Mr. Clive," she replied. She liked the kindly, unassuming young man. He had insisted that they remain in the rectory until they could make other arrangements, and he himself had taken up residence at the Green Dragon, the only inn in the area. "Won't you come in by the fire?"

Smiling, he shook his head. "I will take myself back to the inn now that I am certain things are all right here." He paused a moment in opening the door. "Should I perhaps have someone come back to stay here tonight, Miss Standish?" he asked. "I could have Mrs. Priddy send up one of the ostlers to keep watch."

Marguerite shook her head. "It is kind of you to think of it, Mr. Clive, but Vincent Beezley won't bother us again tonight."

"It might be as well if you did not come to the door again this evening," he observed. "Then you would not put yourself at risk."

"I assure you that I will open the door to no one," Marguerite replied. "Celia and I will be quite secure."

He smiled and said shyly, "And your sister—is she quite all right, do you think? Was she upset by Beezley's intrusion?"

"I am perfectly well, thank you, Mr. Clive," replied Celia softly from the doorway of the library. "Thank you for delivering Marguerite from such an unpleasant situation."

Mr. Clive colored and blinked, taking his spectacles off and nervously placing them in the pocket of his waistcoat. "I was happy to be of service, Miss Celia." He hesitated a moment and then added slowly, "I know that it is none of my business, of course, but you are not thinking of marrying Vincent Beezley, are you?"

Celia shuddered. "No indeed!" she exclaimed. "I would rather wash floors and live in a garret!"

Mr. Clive looked startled by the vehemence of her reaction. "Well, no need for anything quite that drastic, I am certain, but—well, I am glad that you won't consider it."

"You may rest assured that she will not, Mr. Clive," Marguerite replied firmly.

The young man looked relieved, pausing as he reached the door to say, "And if you have any more trouble with

Mr. Beezley, please do inform me of it. I shall take steps to put an end to it."

Marguerite smiled at his firmness. "We shall inform you of it instantly, Mr. Clive."

Reassured, he smiled again and plunged out into the darkness of the storm. Marguerite watched him go, then shut the door firmly and barred it. There would be no more visitors that night. Then she rejoined her sister in the library to resume their sewing.

"Whatever are we going to do, Marguerite?" Celia asked, her voice shaking a little. Her white hands fluttered nervously until she gripped them firmly together in her lap, where they looked still whiter and more fragile against the black muslin of her gown. "It's been more than six months since Papa died, and we can't allow poor Mr. Clive to continue to live at the Green Dragon while we occupy the rectory. If Lady Norwood doesn't wish for us to come to her, what shall we do when we must leave here?"

Marguerite's response was brisk and matter of fact, betraying no indication of her own mounting panic. She knew, even more clearly than Celia, that they would be left without a roof over their heads and without a relative to turn to if Lady Norwood did not invite them to visit her in London. And surely their claim on that lady's generosity was slender enough.

For more nights than she could count she had lain awake for hours, trying to think of reasonable alternatives to living under a hedge when they left the rectory. Fortunately, because of Mr. Clive's kindness they had not already had to face so dire a situation. Smitten by Celia's silvery loveliness and horrified by the desperateness of their plight after their father's unexpected death, he had supplied her with the time necessary to try to find a solution for their problem.

Unfortunately, however, Mr. Clive was soon to marry and might reasonably expect to bring his bride to a home rather than to the Green Dragon Inn, although he had been much too polite to tell them so. If Lady Norwood did not come to their assistance soon, Marguerite must think of something else. She allowed none of her desperation to show in her expression or her tone when she answered her sister, however.

"Why, we shall go out into the world to seek our fortunes, Celia, just as they do in the fairy tales," she replied lightly. "You know that I would make an admirable teacher, and since Mrs. Ruscombe's dear friend is the headmistress of a seminary for young ladies, nothing could be simpler than securing a position with her."

She paused and lifted a quizzical eyebrow at her sister when she did not immediately reply. "You are surely not doubting my ability to teach French, Celia!" she exclaimed. "Not with Mama as a teacher." Here she extended a dainty foot and twirled it. "Or perhaps you feel that I would not be qualified to teach the young ladies how to move gracefully?"

"Of course I don't!" responded Celia, smiling as Marguerite had hoped she would. "There could be no one better suited to teaching than you are, but—"

Marguerite knew that she was about to say what they both were keenly aware of—that Mrs. Ruscombe could be of no help to them now. Their neighbor—and their father's most important parishioner—had suffered a stroke the previous fall which had left her very feeble, with only fleeting periods of coherence. They had grieved over her state before their father's death, but now her loss had become critical, for they had no one else to appeal to save the distant Lady Norwood.

She did not allow Celia to make this bleak observation, but continued quickly. "And you will stay home comfortably and keep the fire and fix me buttered toast and tea when I come home at the end of the day. It will be quite delightful, you and I sitting in front of our own fire. And on Saturday afternoons we will walk in the gardens and visit the shops and perhaps even go to the theater."

Celia's eyes brightened at the cozy picture her sister presented, and for a moment her thoughts were diverted. Only for a moment, however, for her smile faded and she returned to their problem.

"Perhaps we shall be forced to accept Mrs. Blackwell's offer, after all, Marguerite," she sighed.

"We will do no such thing!" her sister replied sharply, her eyes snapping. "How very like Samantha Blackwell to suggest such a cheeseparing thing! Imagine her having the audacity to say that you should be her companion. We both know that she would work you to a bone, making you fetch and carry for her all day long!"

"Well, it would at least give me a roof over my head, Marguerite, so that you don't have to worry about me! Then you could afford to take a teaching position at the seminary because they would provide you with room and board and you wouldn't have the expense of looking after me."

"Yes, I can just imagine it, Celia—my abandoning you to that old harpy, who would make your life miserable and never give you a penny to call your own! We might just as well marry you off to the despicable Vincent Beezley, so that you could work from dawn to dusk for him and bear him three children in the next three years!" She broke her thread off viciously, quite as though she had Mr. Beezley in her grip.

"Marguerite!" exclaimed Celia, shocked by her sister's lack of delicacy.

"You know that what I say is the truth, Celia. Never mind whether it is the proper thing for a lady to speak of. *You* wouldn't be able to speak of it because it is very likely you would be in the churchyard with Mama and Papa at the end of those three years."

Celia wiped away a tear, trying not to call attention to

her action, and Marguerite was immediately filled with compunction. "There now, dear, don't cry. You know that I always speak out of turn. It is what Papa was forever carping about. But it does make me as mad as fire to see people trying to take advantage of you when you are no more than a girl! You would think that the people in Papa's parish would have more respect for his memory!"

"You know that most of them are not in a position to help us, Marguerite. Why, Mrs. Greene cries every time I go there because she is afraid that we will move away soon. She would help us, if she could." She sighed. "If only dear Mrs. Ruscombe were well—although it does seem heartless to wish she were so just for our sakes. The poor lady—lying in her bed day after day and knowing no one."

There was silence for a few minutes, each girl occupied with her own depressing thoughts. When Celia spoke again, she turned to a topic that they had discussed again and again.

"Why do you think Lady Norwood has not responded to our letter? Were not she and our mama bosom bows when they were girls? Why, you were named for her, Marguerite, and she stood godmother to you at your christening."

Even though Celia had asked this question countless times in the past weeks, Marguerite once more answered her patiently. "But that was many years ago, Celia. One-and-twenty to be precise. It's true that we heard from her occasionally until Mama died, but we never saw her once in all those years. Of course," she added fairly, "Mama *was* going to visit her when she was taken with her last illness."

"And poor Lady Norwood was so shocked by her death that she was bedfast for weeks," said Celia, dabbing at her eyes with a small square of linen that was bordered in black. "And she wrote us such a touching letter of condolence when she regained her health."

"And sent us some fruit from her hothouse and that was that," returned Marguerite dryly, less impressed than Celia by Lady Norwood's show of sympathy. "We have had only one brief note since then."

She turned back to her work and plied her needle with vigor, as though doing so would produce another letter from Lady Norwood. "I suspect that she was afraid Papa would apply to them for money," she commented abruptly.

Seeing Celia's wide eyes, she added defensively, "After all, Celia, Papa was only a poor clergyman while Sir Richard Norwood is a very wealthy gentleman with several estates. And Lady Norwood, of course, had it not been for the Terror, would still be living in France. As the daughter of a marquis—and the wife of an important and wealthy man—she has every right to think very well of herself. It is possible that she and Sir Richard did not wish for the connection. That may well be the reason they have not kept in touch nor responded to our letter."

She was reluctant to add the last comment because it would put a period to their hope of assistance, but as the days and weeks had slipped by and no answer to her letter had come, she had been forced to face that possibility.

"That is surely not the case, Marguerite," replied Celia, deeply shocked. "A true friend would not be stopped by such a worldly consideration—and you know that Mama always spoke fondly of her. Indeed, she even said that they were very distant relations—although of course Mama came from a much less important branch of the family. How could she have felt so about Lady Norwood if what you say is true?"

Marguerite smiled at her sister affectionately. "She could do so because she was exactly like you in disposition, my dear goose. She could never see anything wrong in those she loved—indeed, she could not bear to think ill of anyone at all. So I give you leave to defend Lady Norwood, for you cannot help yourself. I wish that I could be half so kind."

Celia's cheeks glowed pinkly at her sister's words and she hastened to defend Marguerite from herself. "It is you that is the goose, Marguerite, for you know that no one could have been kinder and more giving than you have been. You tried to pretend otherwise, but I know what you sacrificed to stay home with me after Mama died so that you could teach me and keep me company."

"You are quite in the right of it," agreed her sister, staring dreamily into the smoldering fire, which was emitting impatient little puffs of smoke, as though it would billow into the room in a mighty cloud of soot if given the least opportunity to do so. "I was entirely overset that I could not accept Mr. Case's proposal of marriage. He was such a taking man and had such address." She sighed deeply as she turned her attention back to the mending in her lap. "It took some months before I could adjust to the loss."

Celia laughed, her silver curls bouncing brightly against the black background of her dress. "How very unkind of you, Marguerite, to make sport of poor Mr. Case," she protested, trying to suppress her laughter. The gentleman in question was most notable for his annoying air of superiority and his unquestionable ability to bore any listener to distraction within a matter of seconds.

Marguerite's eyes twinkled. It was pleasant to see her sister forget her troubles in laughter, even if only for a few moments. Celia had always been sensitive, and she had been distraught over their father's sudden death in a carriage accident. The Reverend Standish had been an aloof, somber man, showing as little emotion to his own daughters as he did to his parishioners and the rest of the world. Only their mother had been able to elicit from him any warmth or cheerfulness.

Nonetheless, Celia's nature was an affectionate one, encompassing even Papa. His loss, coupled with their nearly penniless state and the knowledge that they must soon move from the old rectory, the only home they had ever known, had taken their toll on Celia's gentle spirit. There had been times recently when Marguerite had feared that her sister might not be strong enough to withstand the strain under which they were living. Although nothing seemed to detract from her loveliness, she had grown thinner, and there were faint purple shadows under her eyes.

"It is all very well for you to laugh, my girl," said Marguerite, assuming an air of gravity as she attended carefully to her stitches. "You are not the one who had to listen to him explain how great an honor it would be to become the third Mrs. Edward Case and to look after all the little Cases. It took me the better part of an hour to convince him that I was not worthy of such an honor."

"And it took you much longer than that to convince Papa that you would not accept the offer," added Celia, suddenly grave. "But I know that Mrs. Ruscombe offered to send you to that seminary where you spoke of teaching, and that you would have dearly loved to go. And I know that you received other, more eligible, marriage offers, but would not accept them either. You did that for me so that I wouldn't be left alone." Celia took her sister's hand and pressed it gratefully, and the two girls exchanged a look of understanding.

It was true that Marguerite had received several offers of marriage. Her bright eyes and lively mind endeared her to those about her, and, in at least three instances, her charm had outweighed the disadvantages of her very small marriage portion and her very quick tongue. It was just as true that Marguerite had unhesitatingly refused all offers without a pang of regret. Apart from Mr. Case, the gentlemen in question, while pleasant enough, had been uniformly dull and placid, their lives and conversation tied to the small world in which they lived. Certainly none of them had held any claim upon her heart. And, being of a practical turn of mind, she was well aware that the lively manners that charmed them now would grow less charming in the routine of everyday living. She shuddered at the mere thought of being confined to such a routine for a lifetime.

In truth, the only refusal that had caused her real pain had been the one to Mrs. Ruscombe, for she *had* longed to attend the seminary and to leave the village of Northaven behind her. As it was, she had done her best, with the aid of the kindly Mrs. Ruscombe, to educate herself and Celia at home, continuing the work begun by their mother. Woven through the lessons were the stories Marguerite had gleaned from the well-traveled Mrs. Ruscombe and from reading books and magazines borrowed from her library, which had given her a glimpse of a different world, a world in which conversations did not revolve around the crops and hunting and local gossip.

Her father had been unable to understand her reasons for not marrying and she had not really attempted to explain herself, but Celia had understood. Their mother, a tiny, gentle woman, had provided all the love and warmth for the family. Their father had always been a distant, austere man, and after his wife's death he had become even more withdrawn. It had been in a moment of weakness that he had met and married the charming Angelique D'Arcy, and he had never quite forgiven himself for allowing his emotions to override his judgment on that one occasion. He, who had needed to marry a woman who was serious and practical to aid him in his ministry, had married a young woman with a frivolous upbringing who had no training in the household arts. She was well educated, it was true, but then he did not value education for women. The fragile Frenchwoman had brought her gracious ways to the grim old rectory, and she had provided the loving atmosphere in which her daughters had been reared.

When she died, Marguerite had taken it upon herself to provide the same warmth for her young sister, and she had successfully shielded Celia from most of their father's joyless strictures and had brought what happiness she could into their daily lives. She had found entertainment in the everyday things of life—the people encountered, the small daily chores performed, the books read.

Papa had disapproved strongly both of her desire to learn and her lively ways. He had not allowed either of his daughters to attend the public balls or local assemblies; they had, in fact, attended only a few private parties in the neighborhood, and those despite his disapproval, for he had felt that their time should be employed solely with housekeeping duties and the doing of good works. He had disapproved equally strongly of the time that they spent in their studies, for, as he had noted dourly, they would have little call for them in their lives as wives and mothers—or as dutiful daughters keeping house for their father. Had Mrs. Ruscombe not been an important and wealthy member of his parish, Marguerite was certain that he would have happily ignored her advice and assistance in the rearing of his daughters after the death of his wife. She was profoundly grateful to Mrs. Ruscombe, for she had opened doors for them, making Marguerite aware of worlds that she hadn't even known existed.

Marguerite had willingly borne the brunt of his disapprobation, for she was the elder and more forceful of the sisters, and she had been determined that Celia should have some chance for a happy, normal life. It was with that end in view that she had written to Lady Norwood soon after their father's death, explaining their position and asking her advice since they had no relatives to turn to. She had fervently hoped that they would be invited to London for a visit, for without such a favor, their future looked bleak indeed. With it, she felt that they might reasonably be able to introduce Celia to the *ton* and to find her a husband who, unlike Vincent Beezley, would appreciate her and care for her properly. She knew that under the auspices of Lady Norwood, they would have entrance to all of the best drawing rooms in London, and Marguerite was certain that her sister's remarkable beauty would win countless hearts.

It was from Mrs. Ruscombe that she had learned of what she disparagingly called the marriage market, and of how commonplace it was for a young woman to marry well simply in order to save her family. Now that Celia was seventeen and of an age to wed, Marguerite feared that she might marry someone like Vincent Beezley simply to make life simpler for her sister. Marguerite had no desire to sacrifice Celia, but she feared for her health and well-being and they had very few options available to them. If they could meet some eligible young men, friends of Lady Norwood's in London, Celia might very well meet someone with whom she could be very happy. Whatever happened, she was determined that Celia be properly cared for. Surely it would not be too much to ask for one handsome, wealthy, kindly young man for her.

It was not in Marguerite's nature to give way to despair easily, but as the weeks had passed slowly by with still no word from Lady Norwood, it had been all that she could do to support Celia's failing spirits. Indeed, so desperate had she become that if Mr. Case had again applied for her hand, she would have given the matter serious consideration.

As she brushed her hair and prepared for bed that night, she chuckled grimly to herself, for she realized that she was even thinking of Mr. Alexander Clive as a possible solution to their problem. It was true that he was engaged, and that he seemed much more taken with Celia than with her, but these were matters that could be remedied. And he would at least be able to offer them a home. She did not allow herself to dwell upon the fact that she would be condemning herself to a life spent in Northaven, in the same narrow surroundings that she was attempting to escape.

Pulling the covers up to her chin and closing her eyes with determination, Marguerite allowed herself a final chuckle. Mr. Clive would have had as much trouble sleeping as she if he had known her thoughts. If nothing happened by Saturday, she decided, she would begin a campaign to rearrange Mr. Clive's matrimonial plans.

$\mathcal{T}wo$

Fortunately for Mr. Clive's peace of mind, the morning, like most mornings, particularly those of early spring, brought renewed hope. Last night's storm had washed the world clean, and as Marguerite looked out at the small splashes of color beginning to appear in her mother's beloved garden, she felt her heart lift. It was always at night that she felt most like giving way to despair, and she watched gratefully as a rabbit, nibbling busily at the tender green sprouts just putting in their appearance, paused to regard her seriously before returning to the business of breakfast. As always, with the dawn came sanity and hope. There must, after all, be some way out of this for them.

Deciding that she must keep herself busy while she reviewed their situation for the thousandth time, Marguerite retired to the attic. Although they had taken care of most of Papa's possessions—a duty which had not taken very long since he had not cared much for the things of this world—there were still some boxes and a trunk to sort through. Dealing with dust and cobwebs and setting things in order would help to calm her nerves. Attired in her oldest gown and one of her mother's old caps, she climbed the narrow steps to the attic.

A bright patch of sunlight shone through the dormer window, and she settled herself comfortably in its warmth to open the first box. She had not been able to face doing this in the gray coldness of the winter months, but having light and warmth as company made it all more bearable. She had left Celia below, happily baking bread in the kitchen with Nipper, her canary, for company. There was little point in both of them becoming depressed.

She glanced absently through the first box and then opened the second. Both appeared to be filled with her father's correspondence. He had been an inveterate letter writer and he appeared never to have thrown away a single letter that he had received. Marguerite sighed. There was probably little point in opening each and reading it, but her conscience would not allow her to do otherwise. It seemed rather like prying, but she was certain that the majority, if not all of the letters, would be occupied with church affairs.

And she had been right. Three hours later she dusted her hands wearily on her apron and closed the second box. That would be enough for the moment. The patch of sunlight had disappeared, and with it all warmth and cheerfulness. Reluctantly she opened the lid of the trunk to see what lay within it, braced for the sight of stacks of the rector's carefully penned sermons and voluminous notes on his reading.

To her surprise, the trunk was filled with clothing, carefully packed in brown paper and aromatic bog myrtle to ward off moths. After checking her hands carefully for dust, she turned back a corner of the paper and sighed with pleasure at the sight of a blue silken gown. She stroked the fabric gently. It was Mama's, of course, although she could not recall ever seeing her mother attired in such elegance. No doubt it belonged to the carefree days before she met Papa and became a clergyman's wife. A sudden thought struck Marguerite, and she checked hurriedly below the blue gown to be certain that other contents of the trunk appeared to be in good condition, too. Nothing could be more fortunate! she thought triumphantly, once again certain that there would be a way out of this for them.

Their own clothes were so threadbare that they were scarcely suitable even for wearing into the village, and most certainly they would not answer their needs in London. Marguerite had decided earlier that she would wrestle with only one problem at a time, and since there was no need for fine clothes unless they actually received an invitation to London, she had devoted herself single-mindedly to acquiring the invitation. Now, however, the solution to their wardrobe—or at least to Celia's wardrobe—had fallen into her hands. Celia was most definitely Mama's daughter, as like her in coloring and form and feature as she was in disposition. The colors of the fabrics would be well suited to her, and Marguerite's own nimble fingers could redesign these outdated costumes into the fashionably simple gowns worn today. Her brows drew together as she considered the weight and the old-fashioned design of some of the materials, but she was nonetheless certain that she could manage it.

In an instant she visualized Celia at a London ball, looking ethereal in a gown of white gauze embroidered with silver roses, surrounded by admiring—and eligible— men. For Marguerite had no doubt at all that Celia would be beset by suitors were she only to have the opportunity to move in the proper society. This had been her hope when she had first written to Lady Norwood. There had been no opportunity to seek an invitation from that lady while Papa was still alive, for he would never have permitted it, but after his death it had been not only desirable, but necessary, to attempt to do so.

Marguerite was well aware that Celia could marry and settle in Northaven, for, although she was young, her beauty had always attracted attention. Not for an instant, however, would she countenance her sister's marriage to someone like Vincent Beezley who would consign her to a bleak life with nothing but hard work and numerous children to occupy her. Celia was too delicate for that, and she was not going to sacrifice herself in this dreary little corner of the world.

For a moment longer Marguerite indulged herself with the vision of Celia at the ball, her favorite daydream. She had no doubt that Celia's exceptional beauty and her sweet and biddable disposition would attract a suitable husband who would appreciate her and care for her properly. There was no reason that Celia could not give her heart to a wealthy man as easily as to a poor one.

Once Celia's future was secured, she could look to her own. She had no illusion that she would fare as well as her sister, for her own appeal lay in charm rather than beauty. And what is charming in Northaven is undoubtedly considered insipid and hopelessly provincial in London, my girl, she told herself sternly. So there is no use in puffing yourself up and hoping for anything better.

Resolutely, she stood up to close the lid of the trunk. Once Celia was settled in a new life, she would be able to manage her own future. She could, after all, take a position as a governess or a companion—and, if that seemed rather cheerless, she had best put it from her mind for the time being. Perhaps she could, after all, seek a position in a young ladies' seminary in a town that would at least allow her access to the theater and a respectable library.

As she carefully replaced the blue gown, she noticed a small twist of paper tucked into a corner of the trunk. When she opened it, a blue velvet pouch fell from its folds. Curious, she released the drawstring and moved closer to the window. A heart-shaped locket tumbled onto the palm of her hand and lay glinting in the last ray of sunlight. On its front delicately inscribed initials were intertwined, and Marguerite could distinguish an elaborately scrolled *V* in their midst. On its back was a heraldic rose displaying the five petals of the wild rose, the crest of Lady Norwood's family. Marguerite recalled having first seen it impressed on the wax wafer of a letter her mother had received from Lady Norwood. She had asked its significance at the time and her mother had explained that it was a part of the coat of arms of the de Valencia family. It had seemed curious to her then that Lady Norwood still used the crest from her father's family rather than that of her husband, but Mama had explained briefly that Lady Norwood was very proud of her family and still grieved for their loss during the days of the Terror. Marguerite had seen the symbol again on the wafer of the note of condolence they had received after her mother's death.

She turned the locket back over and traced the *V* lightly with her forefinger. "Marguerite de Valencia," she said slowly, wondering if this could possibly be the help she had been looking for. If it were a locket belonging to Lady Norwood, she would have a legitimate reason to write again to that lady. At this point Marguerite had no illusions about Lady Norwood's charitable notions, but perhaps she would be more eager to see them if they had something that she wanted.

Almost afraid to look inside, she opened the locket and stared at the two delicately tinted miniatures revealed there. She gasped, for the woman's face was so distinctly like that of Mama and Celia that it took her breath away. The gentleman was dark-eyed and smiling, and both had their hair dressed in the elaborate powdered styles of an earlier day.

Marguerite sank slowly to the stool. This must surely belong to Lady Norwood; these were more than likely her parents. How her mother had come to have it she didn't know, but a new and unwelcome thought had occurred to her as she studied the likeness between the lady of the miniature and Mama and Celia. Her mother had seldom spoken of her life in France, and Marguerite had never pressed her, assuming that it made her sad to think of a life and a family that had disappeared with the Revolution.

She had known, of course, that her mother had accompanied Marguerite de Valencia from France just before the Terror. Her father had been the steward of the Marquis de Valencia, and had remained with him. The Marquis had been quite as determined to remain with his estate during the rising storm as he was to remove his only child from possible danger. He had arranged for her to take up residence in London, with Angelique D'Arcy as her companion and an elderly cousin as chaperone. Both young ladies had been little more than girls at the time, but Mama had noted that it was oddly appropriate that they were together. Angelique's mother had accompanied the Marquise from Paris when she had married twenty years earlier.

The elderly cousin who accompanied the girls to London had died shortly after their arrival in London, and the Marquis himself, along with his wife and the parents of Angelique D'Arcy, had perished during the Reign of Terror. Soon afterwards, Marguerite had married Sir Richard Norwood, and Angelique had married the Reverend Samuel Standish and moved to a remote village in the north of England.

To young Marguerite Standish, the story had seemed more a fairy tale than any reality connected with her mother. Now, as she looked at the lovely young face before her, the distant tale became real. If this were truly the Marquise de Valencia, she, along with her dashing husband, had died at the hands of the revolutionaries.

As she studied the miniature, still astounded by the likeness to Celia and her mother, she unwillingly considered the possibility that her mother's relationship to Marguerite de Valencia might have been closer than that of a distant relative. She had read quite enough in Mrs. Ruscombe's library to be aware that it was not unusual for members of the nobility—the French as well as English—to have illegitimate children. The resemblance here was much too striking to be either accidental or distant.

"Perhaps they were half sisters," she mused aloud, comparing the face of the Marquise to that of her memory of her mother, "or cousins." She frowned as she tried to remember the long ago conversation when she had asked her mother about her own parents. Mama had told her that her own mother, whose name was also Angelique, had come from Paris to the estate of the Marquis de Valencia as companion to his bride, Caroline Deauville. That bride would have been the lovely young woman in the miniature.

Could her grandmother and Caroline have looked so much alike, too? Surely not. That would have been too embarrassing for the new Marquise. Angelique's privileged position in the household might have been because she and Caroline shared the same father, however. At any rate, Angelique had accompanied Caroline Deauville into her new world, where she became the Marquise de Valencia, and there Angelique had made her own honorable marriage to the steward of the Marquis.

Marguerite held the miniature closer to the light. Whatever the connection, she thanked heaven for the fact that her mother had kept the miniature. Lady Norwood would surely be interested in seeing this link with her past.

Feeling much more hopeful about their future now, Marguerite tucked the locket into a pocket of her apron and descended the stairs to the kitchen, humming. She would write to Lady Norwood immediately, but she would not tell Celia about her discovery, for she knew that her sister would be shocked by the possibility that Mama had been illegitimate—and Celia needed no more shocks at the moment. Thinking of what their father's reaction to such news would have been, Marguerite shivered inadvertently. Mama had done well to keep such information to herself.

She had quite enough to tell Celia about, however, as she described the rest of the contents of the trunk, and made plans for beginning the refurbishing of their wardrobes. It was a joy to watch the color rise in Celia's face at the pleasure of having some of Mama's dresses for her own. It took a little persuasion to convince her that she could give up her blacks for colors so soon, but Marguerite managed that nicely, pointing out that their black gowns were indeed worn beyond repair and that the little money they had, they must keep. They would make do with the gowns from the trunk. Too, she told Celia that Mama would be disappointed if they did not use her belongings to help themselves.

"And I believe that I shall write to Lady Norwood one more time," she said casually, slicing a piece of Celia's freshly baked bread and spreading it with jam for their tea. "Somehow, Celia, I think that this time we shall hear from her. And when we do," she added gaily, waving the bread knife in the air, "we shall be prepared with a stunning wardrobe, and you shall be the center of attention at every rout we attend."

Celia wiped away the flour from her hands thoughtfully. "I know that you have said so, Marguerite, but I cannot imagine that being the case. I am not clever like you are—I shouldn't know what to say to the gentlemen."

Marguerite smiled at her affectionately. "You have only to be what you are, Celia. You have not only the face of an angel, but the disposition of one as well. How could anyone resist such a combination?"

Celia, who was not fond of praise, colored and turned away to Nipper's cage. "You know that you only say those things because you are my sister, Marguerite," she murmured, stroking Nipper's buttery feathers.

"I know no such thing, dear goose," replied her sister, "and once we are in London, you will see that I am quite in the right of it."

Marguerite had promptly written her letter, this time including the information that she had discovered a locket among her mother's things that she thought must belong to Lady Norwood. She explained that it was inscribed with the rose of the de Valencia coat of arms and that it contained miniatures of a charming couple—the woman looking distinctly like both Marguerite's mama and her sister Celia.

A response came much more quickly than she had expected, and, ripping it open impatiently, she was surprised to see that it was signed by Sir Richard Norwood rather than his wife. He informed them very briefly that he would arrive in two weeks' time to escort them to London. The letter was businesslike in tone rather than hospitable, and Marguerite noted that there was no mention of the length of their stay. She was surprised, too, that there was no explanation of why Lady Norwood had not written the letter herself.

Still, she could not find fault with it. They were going to London, and that was what she had prayed for. Celia would have her opportunity to contract a worthy marriage, and she herself would have the opportunity to see something of the world.

To her surprise a second letter arrived two days later— and it was not at all what she had expected. Fortunately, Celia was not at home when it arrived, having walked down the lane to take old Mrs. Greene a loaf of her bread and a jar of broth. Caring for Papa's flock was still a part of her daily labors.

The wafer on this letter bore neither the heraldic rose nor Sir Richard's crest. Instead, the seal was a rather shapeless blob of red wax. As she scanned the page hastily, the color drained from her face and she sat down on a bench in the entryway.

There was no signature to this letter, and its contents were startling. The writer warned them not to think of coming to Norwood House in London because it would be a dangerous place for them. That would have been quite enough to distress Marguerite, but it ended with the cryptic comment: *Remember what happened to your mother.* Mystified, she folded the letter and put it away. She would not tell Celia about this, for doing so would only serve to upset her.

Not for a moment could she imagine what the warning meant. What *had* happened to their mother? Had something happened while she was the companion of Lady Norwood in those long ago days in London? Puzzle over it as she would, she could think of no reasonable interpretation of the statement, nor could she think of any reason that Norwood House should be dangerous for them.

She lay awake for a very long time that evening, staring out her window at the thin sliver of moon hanging golden in the night sky. If anything should happen to Celia because they went to Norwood House despite this warning, she knew that she would bear the burden of it all her life. Still, if they did not go, she had no possible way to care for her sister. The twin specters of Vincent Beezley and Mrs. Blackwell rose before her, reminding her of other possible fates for her delicate sister. She shook her head sharply to dispel them. Surely she could be alert enough to keep trouble at bay. After all, she had done so successfully for the past six years.

One thing was certain, however. Celia *would* be properly cared for and they would *not* be denied their chance in London because some unknown person attempted to frighten her. This was their golden opportunity and fear would not keep her from taking it. She fell asleep that night with the locket clutched in her hand, a sort of talisman against trouble.

Three

When Marguerite looked at the warning note again the next morning, her bravado of the night before almost melted away. She had very nearly convinced herself that she had been the victim of her own active imagination and that the bright light of morning would show that she had nothing to worry about, but the reality of the crudely written letter forced her to face the fact that someone disliked or feared them enough to do such a thing as this.

Celia was again out of the house, and Marguerite had taken advantage of her absence to take the note out and look at it more carefully in the sunlight provided by the open door. To her dismay, a shadow suddenly fell over the letter, and she looked up to see Mr. Clive standing there. She folded the letter hastily and pushed it into her pocket.

"Excuse me for startling you, Miss Standish," he apologized, looking as surprised by her reaction as his habitually mild expression would allow. "I didn't realize that you hadn't noticed me coming up the drive."

"Forgive me for being so skittish, Mr. Clive," she returned, trying to recover her poise. "I suppose it's just the excitement of getting ready to leave."

He nodded understandingly, then added hesitantly, "I trust that you would tell me, Miss Standish, if you were having any more trouble from Mr. Beezley?"

"Of course I would," she assured him, grateful to have the conversation on safer ground. "Vincent Beezley has been no problem at all. And we do appreciate your help very much. Now that he knows that you are aware of his behavior, I am certain that he will think twice before behaving so poorly."

Mr. Clive's complexion grew pink at her praise, and he smiled diffidently. "I was glad to be of service to you and your sister." He hesitated a moment, then added, "I trust that you know, Miss Standish, that you and Miss Celia could call upon me at any time—even after you leave Northaven—if I could be of any help to you."

"That's very kind of you, Mr. Clive," she replied sincerely, thinking that the new Mrs. Clive was unlikely to approve of such an offer.

"I realize that you will be with your mother's friends in London, and that you will be quite out of the sphere of a humble clergyman, but I am to be depended upon should you need me, ma'am."

"I am certain of it," said Marguerite, shaking hands with him firmly. She was happy to think that he and his wife would be settling at the rectory. Under his kindly eye it would be a pleasant place again, with the cheerfulness that had been lost after her mother's death. She hoped that the new Mrs. Clive appreciated his true value.

After this encounter Marguerite put the note away, successfully blocking all thought of the warning from her mind, and the days left to them before the arrival of Sir Richard passed in a bustle of cheerful activity. Every gown and length of lace in Mama's trunk was taken out, exclaimed over, and carefully scrutinized to determine how it could be best employed. In record time they managed to provide Celia with a reasonable wardrobe and even Marguerite gained a gown or two. The fact that they had been Mama's provided the girls with a little more courage than they might have had otherwise, for she had been elegant even in a plain kersey gown.

Even Nipper seemed to be aware of the change in atmosphere, and he gave unceasing voice to his approval of the situation from the time the cover was removed from his cage in the morning until the time Celia re-covered him at night.

"I hope that he doesn't catch a cold on the trip to London," Celia remarked, eyeing her pet with concern on their last evening but one in the old rectory. Again they sat by the fire sewing, setting the finishing touches on their gowns. Nipper had paused in his serenade to preen himself daintily, as though he, too, was aware that appearances count for much in this life. "It is still very chilly, and drafts won't be good for him. Even though the house is cold, I know the warm corners and the best places to keep him. He is quite used to it here."

Marguerite had been dreading this conversation and had postponed it for days, for she knew how fond Celia was of her canary. Doing her best to choose her words carefully, she replied, "You are right, of course, about the drafts, and we *wouldn't* want anything to happen to him, Celia. Old Mrs. Greene is terribly fond of him, you know. Had you considered leaving him with her?"

Celia stared at her, puzzled. "To take care of him, do you mean?" She thought for a moment. "But, Marguerite, remember that we are not coming back here. That is why you told Mr. Clive that you would send for the boxes that we are leaving in the attic."

"Yes, I know, dear, but—" Marguerite broke off and stirred uneasily under Celia's shocked gaze.

"I know that you can't mean that I would leave Nipper forever, Marguerite! I couldn't go away and leave him all alone! Why, he is a part of the family! He even knew Mama!"

Nipper looked up brightly, quite aware that he was the subject of conversation, and then threw back his head and trilled joyfully.

"There! He knows that we're talking about him, Marguerite. You see that I can't abandon him. Why, he would very likely waste away and die if we left him behind." Celia's voice was pleading.

Marguerite relinquished her attempt and hoped that Sir Richard would be a more understanding man than his letter had indicated. From what she had observed of men, few of them would be entranced by the thought of having a canary as a traveling companion and subsequently as a house guest. Instead, she turned the conversation to the anticipated delights of their visit.

"What do you suppose it will be like in London?" asked Celia dreamily. "Do you suppose that we shall go riding in the park?"

"I am sure that we shall," returned Marguerite, who had not the slightest idea what their life with the Norwoods would be like. "There will be more things to do and see than we can imagine at the present moment. But, most important of all, Celia," she added, shaking out the skirt of the lilac gown she had been working on, "we shall find you a delightful husband and a home of your own." She had spent the past few days trying to convince Celia of the benefits of marrying well.

Celia's face clouded. "I know that it is important, Marguerite, and that all the things you say about needing a home are true and that we must be practical—even though it does seem so worldly—and so—so *businesslike*. I think, though, that I would be much more comfortable if Nipper and I kept house for you while you taught at the seminary."

Marguerite hugged her. "Don't be a goose, Celia! You shall not marry unless you wish to—but I daresay that you will meet some charming and eligible young gentleman who quite sweeps you off your feet."

Celia still looked dubious, and so she added comfortingly, "And I do promise, dear heart, that if that doesn't happen, we shall do just as you wish and set up housekeeping together. And if the young gentleman *does* happen along, why I shall come and visit you with regularity."

"Come and visit us!" exclaimed Celia. "Why, it would be no such thing! You would live with us, of course. How could I bear to be parted from you, Marguerite?"

She sat for a moment, clearly deep in thought, and then her face brightened. "But how wonderful that would be, Marguerite! I hadn't truly thought about it, but if I should marry and have a home of my own, then I could take care of you just as you have done for me!"

She straightened up, looking determined, and held the lilac gown under her chin. "You must show me what to say and how to act, Marguerite. I know that we must have a roof over our heads. I shall indeed find a husband and we shall all be very happy together!"

Grateful that her thoughts had taken a more cheerful turn, even if the husband-to-be in Celia's pretty picture was clearly no more than a necessary piece of furniture, Marguerite hugged her again. The girls then gave themselves to their handiwork with renewed vigor, turning their conversation to Sir Richard Norwood and speculations about what that gentleman would be like.

"I expect he will give himself airs," said Marguerite, as she retrimmed an old chip bonnet with care. "After all, he is exceedingly wealthy and he must think it quite beneath him to make this long journey for two penniless girls."

"Perhaps not!" protested Celia. "After all, Marguerite, he *is* making the journey, and it is quite a long one. It's good of him to do so when you know that he would not have been traveling in this direction for any other reason."

Marguerite was forced to concede that, for Northaven did not lie on the road to any place of consequence, but she remained firm in her opinion of what he would be like. She was certain that he would be tall, with iron gray hair—very distinguished and very aloof. And, as it happened, she was quite in the right of it—with one notable exception.

When the brisk knock that they had been expecting finally sounded at the door the next afternoon, Marguerite opened it brightly, but her carefully rehearsed words of welcome died upon her lips. The man standing there had hair as dark as midnight and he was certainly not of an age to be Sir Richard Norwood.

"I beg your pardon, sir," she apologized. "I was expecting someone else. May I help you?"

The dark-haired man at the door gazed down at her impassively, no light of greeting in his eyes. "If you are Miss Marguerite Standish, you certainly may," he responded, showing no more expression in his tone than in his face. "I am Sir Richard Norwood."

Marguerite stared at him. He was a square-shouldered, dark-visaged man in a greatcoat with countless capes and he seemed to fill the doorway and block out the spring sunlight. The size of some gentlemen was reassuring, as though offering a measure of protection to those who stood in their shadow. It was not so with this man. For a moment, the warning note came darkly to mind. There was no doubt in her mind that this man could be a threat. To her irritation, Marguerite found herself taking a step back into the entryway.

"You are Sir Richard!" she exclaimed, wondering at his age and dismayed by the coldness of his expression. Then she caught herself and attempted to speak with a measure of dignity. "Forgive my lack of manners, sir," she added stiffly. "Please do come into the library."

As she took Sir Richard's coat and hat and led him to a low chair by the fire, she tried to explain her outburst, saying lightly, "I had expected an older man, you see, for I knew that Lady Norwood and my mother were of an age."

"You were expecting my father then, Miss Standish, and he has been dead these several years. Lady Norwood is my stepmother."

"I am sorry to have been taken so much by surprise,

Sir Richard," Marguerite responded, feeling more awkward by the minute, "and sorry for your loss as well. I had no knowledge of your father's death."

"You and Lady Norwood were not in contact at that time?" he inquired shortly, his piercing gaze making her more uncomfortable still. He reminded her of a hawk, his dark brows oddly winged above fierce eyes that seemed almost tawny in color because of their countless flecks of gold.

"No. Your stepmother has not corresponded with us since the death of our mother six years ago." She cast about, trying to think of something to say to this abrupt, uncomfortable man. "It is most kind of you to make this journey to escort my sister and me to London." Her voice sounded weak, even to her own ears.

He did not acknowledge her thanks, but merely said shortly, "We shall not be in London long, Miss Standish, merely a few days. We shall then be going directly to Bath."

Marguerite's face fell. Bath! That was a far cry from the glories of London. And there would most certainly be fewer eligible men for Celia. Even Marguerite knew that Bath was no longer the most fashionable of watering-holes for the *ton*.

Sir Richard studied her, a faint glimmer of malice lighting his amber eyes. "Does that not suit with your plans, Miss Standish?" he inquired. "Perhaps you were looking forward to something more exciting?"

"May I ask what takes you to Bath, Sir Richard? Do you plan to take the waters?" she asked, ignoring his tone and his questions and deciding to be just as abrupt as he. The fact that he was quite correct in his assumption scarcely put her more in charity with him. And never, she thought bitterly, had she seen anyone less in need of taking the waters for his health.

He did not rise to the bait, probably merely amused that she would attempt to irritate him. Instead, he said briefly,

"Lady Norwood has been ill, and I am to take her there to recuperate. You and your sister will of course accompany her."

How could anything be worse, Marguerite wondered, hoping devoutly that she was not further exposing her dismay to this ungracious man. It was clear that he was enjoying her discomfiture. Covering her displeasure as best she could, she attempted to look properly concerned, saying coolly, "Naturally we will. I only hope that we may be of service to her."

"I feel certain that you will be," he said dryly. "Lady Norwood will see to that."

It grew worse and worse with each comment he made. Marguerite envisioned them becoming little more than unpaid companions to a querulous, demanding invalid, subject to her every whim and forced to endure every sort of slight. A wrenching thought struck her: was this what the anonymous note meant? That she and Celia would end as companions to Marguerite de Valencia as their mother had?

She was suddenly aware that Sir Richard was speaking to her. "As I was saying, Miss Standish, perhaps you and your sister might be happier elsewhere than in Bath with my stepmother. Have you no one else who might be of service to you?"

"No," she replied bleakly, seeing little point in concealing the way matters stood. "I speak quite frankly, Sir Richard, when I say that if Lady Norwood had not sent for us we would be in desperate straits when the new rector moves in here."

"And what shall you do when your visit with Lady Norwood is over?" he asked abruptly, his face darker than ever.

Angered by his tone, Marguerite straightened her shoulders and glared at him. "We shall manage very well, Sir Richard. We are not expecting to live on your coattails, if that is what you are asking."

He looked surprised by her plain speaking, but his next

question made it clear that he did not for a moment believe her. "Indeed? And I suppose you and your sister will be like the fabled Gunning sisters and take London—or, in this case, Bath—by storm?"

Marguerite's cheeks reddened. "You forget yourself, sir," she said sharply. "My sister and I are gentlewomen, although our state, as you can see," and here she waved her hand to indicate their shabby surroundings, "is far from the kind of elegance to which I am certain that you are accustomed." She did not feel it necessary to share with the fact that she did indeed expect Celia to take London—or Bath—by storm.

He did not reply, but continued to study her coolly, an attitude scarcely calculated to conciliate her.

"I must thank you, Sir Richard, for an unexpected insight you have offered me. I had not before realized that genteel poverty offered any advantages," she said, her smile sweet as she added, "but it at least has not allowed us to believe that we may ride roughshod over others."

If she had intended to shame him, she had failed. His expression did not alter. "And I suppose that was intended to put me properly in my place, Miss Standish. I applaud you. You have rehearsed your part well and you mean to take advantage of your opportunities. I suppose that I would do the same if I found myself in your position."

Before she could retort, he held his hand up to stop her and added, "And I would merely add that if you have any other choice as to your course of action, it would be wiser than the one you are taking. Do not expect anything from us beyond your visit in Bath."

Marguerite was a little shaken by his words, which seemed to go beyond the bounds even of rudeness. Why would he warn her against going to Lady Norwood? Because he did not wish to be burdened with the expense of them? Because he thought they would become hangers-on, living on the fringes of the household? Or was there something else behind his words? For a wild moment she tried to imagine the arrogant Sir Richard lowering himself to write the anonymous note, but she could not picture it. He would have signed it proudly and phrased it as an order rather than a warning.

Before she could say anything, the door opened and Celia came shyly in, carrying with her Nipper's cage. Although she would never have had the courage to ask a favor for herself, for the sake of her pet she was willing to face the lion. She made a fetching picture in her lilac gown, her silver hair caught up with ribbons of the same shade, but Marguerite groaned inwardly, certain that Sir Richard was about to sharpen his teeth on her hapless young sister. Grimly she introduced them, and braced herself as Celia held up the cage for Sir Richard to inspect her pet.

"Forgive me for troubling you, Sir Richard, when you have been so kind as to come all this distance for us. I know that Marguerite thinks it would be an imposition to ask to take Nipper with us," she said earnestly, "and I *am* afraid that he might not be warm enough, but indeed, Sir Richard, I *cannot* abandon him. How could I explain to him that he must be left with someone else after being with me for seven years? It is asking a great deal, I know, but—"

To Marguerite's amazement he replied in a tone that was almost gentle. "Not at all, Miss Celia. Of course you must honor the trust that your pet has in you. I am surprised that your sister would have you do such an unfeeling thing— although it is, of course, the practical thing to do." His tone indicated that he felt no surprise at all, however. Undoubtedly, Marguerite reflected with some annoyance, it was precisely what he would have expected of her.

"Oh, Marguerite would never be unkind, Sir Richard," responded Celia quickly. "But she did not wish to inconvenience you or Lady Norwood."

Sir Richard glanced at Marguerite, his dark eyebrows

lifted. "Sometimes there are obligations that must be met—even if one fears that the result will be inconvenient."

No doubt that was an oblique reference to the inconvenience that the two of them were causing him, thought Marguerite, growing more irritated with each comment he made. And he probably felt that she was being considerate of him only because she did not wish to endanger their chances of making the visit.

"I assure you, Miss Standish, that we shall see to—" and here he paused to glance down at the tiny bird, trying to recall its name "—to Nipper's comfort in the chaise. He will come to no harm on our journey."

"Thank you, Sir Richard," Celia replied, setting down the cage on the elderly tea table. "Do let me introduce you to Nipper."

And to her sister's horror, Celia proceeded to extricate Nipper from his cage and, once having him perched on her forefinger, inveigled him to hop upon the sleeve of Sir Richard's impeccable dark blue jacket. Marguerite closed her eyes, fearing the worst, for Nipper did not always remember his manners. To her relief, however, the only damage done to the gentleman's raiment was a dusting of pale gold feathers.

The reasons for his unexpected kindness seemed clear to Marguerite. The first and most satisfying was that Celia's beauty and artlessness had had exactly the effect upon him that they had on most gentlemen. She seemed to elicit chivalrous behavior, even in one as totally lost to good manners as Sir Richard. The second one was less palatable to her. He had, she thought, cast *her* as a heartless social climber, a woman with no finer feelings who would thoughtlessly sacrifice her young sister's happiness for the sake of ingratiating herself with him and Lady Norwood. Angry though she was, however, she could not bring herself to say anything when she looked at Celia's glowing face. She managed to meet Sir Richard's gaze coolly and to echo her sister's thanks.

"Sir Richard has been telling me that we will be in London only briefly and then will be going directly to Bath," Marguerite said to her sister. "Lady Norwood has been ill and is going to take the waters."

"How dreadful, Sir Richard," responded Celia warmly, her eyes filled with concern. "And here we are causing you to be called away at such a time! But at least we will be able to help Lady Norwood instead of merely being guests. We have had some experience helping Papa with his parishioners when they were ill."

"I am certain that Lady Norwood will appreciate your sentiments, Miss Celia," replied Sir Richard, glancing at Marguerite as though in no doubt as to *her* sentiments on the subject.

"We would, naturally, wish to be of what assistance we could," said Marguerite, well aware that her tone lacked sincerity. She had a dismal picture of their future as a constant round of digestive biscuits and camomile tea and chicken broth.

"How very kind he is," sighed Celia after Sir Richard had departed for the Green Dragon to have his dinner.

Marguerite looked at Celia in amazement. It was true that Sir Richard had been quite cordial to her, in marked contrast to his treatment of Marguerite, but of course Celia had not witnessed that portion of his behavior. And she was grateful for that, she told herself, since there was little point in upsetting Celia if she were disposed to look kindly upon the gentleman. It would make their journey— and perhaps their entire visit—more pleasant for her.

As for Marguerite, she could not decide what to think of him. He had been unquestionably—and unaccountably—rude to her. He seemed to have taken her in instant dislike. And she could not decide, as she thought back through their conversation later that evening, whether or not there had been anything ominous in his behavior or if that feeling were attributable entirely to his forbidding appearance. It was possible, of course, that the anonymous note had been meant to warn her about Sir Richard. Why she should be warned about him—since bad manners were scarcely reason enough—was another question.

She put the question out of her mind for their last evening at home. Arm in arm, the girls walked through the old rectory and into their mother's garden.

"I do hope that Mr. Clive's bride is fond of gardens," remarked Celia wistfully, as they admired the snowdrops in the gentle twilight. "Mama worked so hard on this one that it should be kept as she intended it to be."

"I'm sure that they will take good care of it," Marguerite comforted her. "Just as they will watch over Mama's ducks and geese that you have cared for all these years. Doubtless there will soon be several little Clives who will feed them at dawn and watch them floating on the pond at twilight, just as we always have."

Celia smiled at the picture her sister had conjured. It always satisfied her to think that other people would enjoy the same quiet pleasures that she did. Nor was she selfish, as Marguerite remarked to herself in amazement for the hundredth time. With the notable exception of Nipper, if Celia could not have something, she did not begrudge the having to someone else—indeed, she seemed to find a sort of vicarious pleasure in it, something that Marguerite had never been able to understand.

She sighed. Surely there would be someone who would appreciate Celia at her true value—if not in London, then in Bath. Perhaps the quieter atmosphere there would be better suited to her gentle sister than would the fast pace of London.

Together they went down to the little churchyard where their parents lay side by side and placed a bouquet of snowdrops from the garden on their graves. Marguerite had tried to pay the elderly sexton for the upkeep of the graves after they left, but he had refused her money, assuring her that he would take care of the reverend and his wife for no fee at all and wishing them Godspeed on their journey. "You will be needing your money, and it is little enough that I can do for your mother after all that she did for my daughter before she died," he had said firmly, his kindness bringing tears to Marguerite's eyes.

When they returned to the rectory, they went up to their chambers to do their final packing, and together they watched the last pink flood of sunset melt into darkness. Before snuffing her candle that night, Marguerite took out the locket again and opened it, finding comfort in the tender expression of the young woman in the miniature. It was so like looking at Mama and Celia.

Closing it gently, she wondered if Lady Norwood too would bear a striking resemblance to them. Perhaps she would find that Lady Norwood was very like them in temperament as well. On that pleasant thought, she drifted off to a peaceful sleep, for the first time in many nights hopeful about their future. Not even the face of Sir Richard or the specter of warning notes had the power to interrupt her slumber.

Four

True to his word, Sir Richard was at the rectory at an early hour the next morning and made the ladies comfortable in the chaise while their baggage was secured. Much to Celia's pleasure, Nipper received special consideration, for Sir Richard personally placed his cage on a pillow to lessen the jolting of the carriage, and then strapped it carefully into position next to her, at the last using a lap robe as a tent over it and a footwarmer placed just below the seat so that its warmth would rise to the cage.

"Never was a bird so pampered!" exclaimed Marguerite, pleased that her sister's pet was receiving such attention. It surprised her a little that Sir Richard would take such pains, but now that she was once again in the bright and cheerful light of morning, she supposed that she had been too quick in her judgment of him. That was one of her failings, she knew. She was inclined to make hasty first assessments and then revise them at her leisure.

"I believe that this is the first time my chaise has had such a passenger," commented Sir Richard. "I trust that he will find his accommodations satisfactory."

"If he does not," retorted Marguerite, "you may be certain that we shall all be informed of it. Nipper does not keep his feelings a secret."

Celia laughed at the exchange, her curls bright against the darkness of her pelisse. Seeing her happiness, Marguerite felt more certain than ever that they were doing the proper thing, and she settled back against the soft velvet squabs of the seat to enjoy the journey.

The arrangement of their seats within the chaise was a comfortable one. Both of the seats faced forward, and Sir Richard had seated himself in front and the girls and Nipper on the second bench. This was a considerate arrangement, for there were few things Marguerite disliked more than feeling she was being scrutinized, as she would have had he been seated behind them. As it was, she could observe the back of his head to her heart's content and be untroubled by such scrutiny herself. She had been correct in her first startled assessment yesterday: his hair was black, as black as a raven's wing, with the same glossiness. And he was as arrogant and ominous as one she told herself. It really did not matter that his appearance was striking when his manner left so much to be desired.

Fortunately, none of them felt compelled to talk, and the morning passed quickly enough, the familiar countryside slipping away from them and new scenes offering themselves. Nipper and Celia dozed quietly in the comfort of the warm, well-sprung chaise, and Sir Richard appeared to be occupied by his own thoughts. When they stopped to change horses, he helped them down, showed them into a private dining room of the posting inn, and ordered a light meal for them. He took his own refreshments in the coffee room.

"It would have been more polite of him to have joined us," observed Marguerite. "This makes it appear that he does not wish to spend any more time with us than is necessary."

"I am certain that it is more comfortable for him to be in the coffee room, Marguerite, where he can visit with other gentlemen and drink something a little stronger than he might partake of with us," said Celia soothingly. "And he has certainly been a thoughtful host, looking after all out needs."

Marguerite was aware that she was being petty, but it did seem to her that it would have been more gentlemanly to offer them his company than merely to see to their comfort. Not, of course, that she had any particular complaints about their treatment on the journey thus far. Aside from his lack of interest in their company, he had been very attentive to their care. What more could she ask? Even Nipper is being better tempered than you are, she scolded herself. It was unfortunate that Sir Richard seemed to see the worst in her, for she appeared to be equally obliged to show him that he was quite right in his estimate in her character.

She returned to the chaise with an air of quiet determination, every inch a stoic, steeling herself to be pleasant. Once seated, she weakened and almost succumbed to the temptation of trying to engage him in idle chatter, something that she was certain he would detest, just to assure him that his assessment of her character had been quite correct. However, she heroically rose above it and took out a slim volume entitled *Sense and Sensibility* to occupy herself. It had been a gift from Mrs. Ruscombe after her last journey to London. She had read it several times, but she was again captured at once by the plight of the Dashwoods, reminding her so markedly of their own, and the afternoon flew by without her once attempting to bait Sir Richard.

When the chaise tooled smartly into the courtyard of the posting house where they were to stay the night, Marguerite gasped as she saw the sign. The Rose and Thistle! She glanced sharply at Celia, who had also seen it and grown pale. There could scarcely have been a less auspicious choice. This was the inn where their mother had died.

Marguerite could still remember vividly the day the message had arrived for their father, brought by one of the posting boys from the inn. She had watched Papa read it and then crumple it in his hand. All he had said to her was "Your mother is dead, Marguerite. I must go and make the arrangements." And she and Celia had been left to comfort one another while the sexton had hurried over to Mrs. Ruscombe's manor with the news.

Papa had brought her home and buried her in the tiny churchyard where he now lay beside her. The service had been on a late afternoon in early spring, a pale golden day much like today. Papa had thrown a handful of earth on her coffin as it lay in the grave, but the girls had strewn dried rose leaves from Mama's own garden, their fragrance lingering in the evening air. It had been too early for the roses, of course, but Marguerite had remembered the jars of dried rose leaves that Mama had kept for making her potpourri. Papa had not approved, naturally, feeling that it was too frivolous a gesture, but Marguerite had not cared. Mama would have liked it.

She had managed to piece together some of the story of what had happened. Mama had gone to the inn to meet Lady Norwood. It was to have been a joyful occasion, their first time to meet in many years, but it had ended in tragedy when her mother collapsed, the victim of heart failure. Lady Norwood, never strong herself, had had to remain several days at the inn under the care of a doctor before she could return to her home. They had received the one letter of condolence from her and, as she had told Celia, that had been that. Lady Norwood had clearly wished to sever ties with the Standishes once her friend was dead.

For a moment Marguerite wondered what Lady Norwood's reaction to the news of the locket had been, but then she remembered that lady's illness and wondered if she *had* read it. Perhaps Sir Richard had been the one to read it and make a decision. And she wondered, too, why they had been invited so quickly to visit after her second letter when there had been no response at all to the first. Of course, if Lady Norwood had been ill for some time that might explain it. The first letter could have simply been overlooked.

She and Marguerite entered the inn reluctantly, their pleasure in their first evening gone. If Sir Richard noticed any change in their demeanor, he did not comment upon it, but turned them over to the maid to be led to their chambers. After resting briefly and changing their gowns, they were invited to join him for dinner in a private dining room below.

The dinner was excellent and after their own simple daily fare, Marguerite and Celia were quite overcome by the number of dishes: hare soup, removed by boiled turbot and lobster sauce, a compote of pigeons and larded sweet-breads, ducklings and wine jelly. Showing the proper deference to a gentleman of Sir Richard's quality, the innkeeper ushered them into their dining room and they were served by the innkeeper's wife herself, a rosy little personage dressed in a sateen gown of cherry stripes. Marguerite had noticed her when they first entered The Rose and Thistle; she had been chatting volubly with two of the other guests. Now, however, she was silent, apparently a tribute both to Sir Richard's rank and to his demeanor, which was, as usual, forbidding.

On an impulse, Marguerite turned to her as she was removing the veal scallops and replacing them with an aspic. "Excuse me, ma'am," she said, catching the good lady's eye. "Have you and your husband had this inn for a very long time?" She carefully avoided Sir Richard's eye, for she was certain that he would disapprove of speaking to the servants in such a manner.

The innkeeper's wife was clearly surprised at being addressed, but she replied readily enough, her voice filled with pride. "For fourteen years Mr. Hammond and I have owned The Rose and Thistle, miss. And it is the finest posting-house in this part of the country. Ask anyone between here and London and they will tell you."

"I'm certain that it is a fine inn and you are very right to be proud of it," returned Marguerite warmly. "What I wished to ask you, however, since you have been here so long, is whether or not you were present six years ago this spring when a lady took ill and died here."

It would have been difficult to have determined who looked the more surprised, Mrs. Hammond or Sir Richard. His eyebrows arced and he paused in the act of raising his glass to his lips.

Mrs. Hammond recovered herself first and replied without hesitation, giving free reign to her tongue as though she could not curb it once she had begun. "Indeed I was here, miss, and a sadder sight you never saw. Why, I served the pretty little thing just before she collapsed. She was talking to the other lady when she suddenly turned scarlet and started dabbing at her forehead with her handkerchief as though she was too warm. She just stopped in the middle of a sentence, and then she started to rise from her chair and clasped her hands to her heart and fell over, all a-heap. Set us on our heels, it did. The other lady that was with her went into hysterics and we had a proper set-to while we got both of them off to bed and sent for the surgeon. The little one that had been taken ill died before he could even get here, and he came as quick as could be."

She clucked and shook her head. "A terrible tragedy it was. Her husband came to collect her the very next day. Very grim, he was, but why shouldn't he have been, losing such a pretty young wife?"

Mrs. Hammond was clearly a chatty soul and had gotten quite caught in her story, but she suddenly looked at Marguerite and Celia more closely. "You have the look of her, miss, if I remember rightly," she said to Celia.

"We are her daughters," said Marguerite quickly, knowing that Celia would be too overcome to speak.

Mrs. Hammond looked suddenly wary. "We did all that

we could for her, miss. Indeed we did. She just went off very suddenlike."

"I am sure that you did all that could be done," replied Marguerite comfortingly. "We simply wanted to know what happened. Our father was never willing to speak of it, and now that he has died, too, we would never have known the circumstances of our mother's death without your kindness."

Reassured by her words, Mrs. Hammond warmed to them, her motherly heart touched by their situation. "I am that sorry, miss, to hear that you have lost your pa, too. I wish that there was more that I had to tell you, but it all happened so quick."

She rubbed her hands on her apron for a moment, appearing to search her memory for any bit of the story she had not shared. "The other lady was taken with hysterics, as I said, and it took me and her maid and two of my chambermaids to get her to her room that night. Took on something terrible she did, until the surgeon came and gave her some laudanum. She told us as how the young lady had been her only real friend and she hadn't seen her for years until just that night. It took several days before she was able to travel back to London, and the surgeon had to come twice a day while she was here."

Marguerite and Celia thanked her again for sharing her memories of the occasion, and Mrs. Hammond, thoroughly softened by their youth and their losses—and their obvious lack of desire to cause trouble—smiled at them in a maternal fashion and assured them that they were more than welcome. She started to leave the dining room but paused and said slowly, "The lady that was her friend said, too, that your mama had had the scarlet fever when they were girls together, and that her heart had been weak ever since."

"Our mother seldom talked of her childhood, Mrs. Hammond, so we had no knowledge of that illness. We merely thought she was fragile in health—we didn't know about her heart."

"Is that so?" responded Mrs. Hammond in wonder. "Well, I can see that it would be something she mightn't have wanted to talk about before her children. Very likely your pa knew of it, though, and simply didn't mention it."

And that would have been very like him, thought Marguerite bitterly. Keeping everything to himself, as though the things that concerned Mama did not concern them all.

Mrs. Hammond finally bowed herself out of the room, reappearing briefly with an apple tart and cheesecakes and coffee.

"I had not realized that I was bringing you to a place that would have such unfortunate memories for you," said Sir Richard, studying them. "I apologize."

"Of course you did not. How could you be expected to know, Sir Richard?" asked Celia in a low voice.

Marguerite said nothing but looked at him steadily. *Had* he known? Had he brought them there deliberately? And, if he had, why would he have done so?

He met her gaze quite as steadily, but she could read nothing more in his expression than his usual absence of emotion.

Later that evening, after Celia was asleep, she slipped downstairs to seek out Mrs. Hammond again. The innkeeper's wife was scandalized to see her out so late in the public area of the inn and hurried her into her own tiny parlor, away from the gaze of any gentlemen who might wander from the taproom. There, amidst a profusion of cabbage roses on the wallpaper and so many dark, heavily carved pieces of furniture that there seemed little room for people, she and Marguerite were seated.

"Now, miss, what has brought you out this time of night?" she inquired, her eyes bright with curiosity.

"I know this will sound foolish, Mrs. Hammond, but I was wondering—I was wondering if you could show me

where my mother was when she was taken ill, and—"
She hesitated over the next words.

"And where she was when she died?" asked Mrs. Hammond, her plump face kind.

Marguerite nodded, and the innkeeper's wife stood up briskly.

"There's no problem with the first one, miss, for that dining room is empty this time of night. The bedchamber is occupied, though."

"Well, I rather expected that," replied Marguerite, her disappointment showing, "so I will make do with just the dining room."

Accordingly, they paid a visit to the small dining room. It was quite plain; there was nothing at all remarkable about it and Marguerite felt a little let down. She wasn't certain what she had expected—but something more than this. A fresh white cloth was on the one table and chairs were ranged stiffly about it. A single still-life of flowers hung over the sideboard and there was one bench under the single latticed window.

Mrs. Hammond watched her with an understanding eye. "It don't seem right—that a death can happen and everything still look so ordinary."

Marguerite nodded her head in agreement, unable for a moment to speak.

"Your mother sat right there," said Mrs. Hammond, pointing to a chair close to the end of the table. "And the other lady—"

"Lady Norwood," volunteered Marguerite.

"That's right!" exclaimed Mrs. Hammond triumphantly. "I was trying to remember her name when I was telling Mr. Hammond about your being here, but I couldn't call it to mind at all. I thought perhaps I would have to get out the register for all that time ago and look it up. At any rate," she continued, remembering what she had been saying, "Lady Norwood was seated just next to your mother, at the very end of the table."

"Mrs. Hammond, did Lady Norwood resemble my mother in appearance?" Marguerite asked hesitantly.

Mrs. Hammond paused to consider the matter, clearly something she hadn't thought about before. "Well," she said slowly, "they both had light-colored hair—although your mother's was more a silvery color like your sister's, while Lady Norwood's was more the color of flax."

"Is there anything else you remember?" asked Marguerite, hungry for every detail.

Mrs. Hammond shook her head. "It's a long while ago, dearie," she apologized. "And, of course, Lady Norwood was dressed very fine, while your mother—well, she was dressed like a lady, but very plain."

Marguerite nodded. Of course she had been. Papa would never have allowed it to be otherwise, even if they could have afforded it. "That's all right, Mrs. Hammond. I appreciate your time."

"Glad to be of help, my dear. I have two girls myself, and I hope that someone would give them the time of day if I was carried off sudden. You and your sister come back to see me whenever you have a mind to."

Marguerite thanked her again, and started up the stairs to her chamber. On the stairs, however, she encountered Sir Richard, who paused and looked down at her as though awaiting an explanation of her presence.

Holding her head high, she sailed past him with a cool nod. "Good night, Sir Richard," she said briefly, not looking back.

"Good night, Miss Standish," he called after her. "I hope that you discovered everything you wished to know."

Her cheeks flushed, she continued to her room as though she hadn't heard him and latched the door behind her. Doubtless he felt superior because he had guessed what she was about. He would probably make it his business to discover just what she had been asking.

She had always thought Papa high-handed, but she could see already that Sir Richard would put him to shame. He seemed to feel it necessary to be in control of those about him, and privy to their every thought. Papa had at least left her to her own thoughts. She hoped that Mrs. Hammond would talk him to death, she thought in irritation as she plumped her pillow with a ferocious thump. It would serve him right.

Five

There was no indication the next morning that her wish had been granted. Sir Richard appeared as unapproachable as ever, exchanging only a few remarks with Celia and ignoring Marguerite altogethcr. While they waited for the chaise to be brought round, Mrs. Hammond appeared on the stairs and beckoned silently to Marguerite, who was standing a little behind the others. She followed the landlady up the stairs just as quietly so that neither Celia nor Sir Richard would notice her departure.

As she had guessed, Mrs. Hammond was taking her to the chamber where her mother had died, the gentleman who had engaged it for the night having already departed. It was a pleasant little room, its chintz-curtained windows overlooking the kitchen garden in the back of the inn. At the moment a striped cat with topaz eyes was curled in comfort on the coverlet, and he regarded tolerantly Mrs. Hammond's vigorous efforts to remove him.

"Dratted cat!" she exclaimed. "He thinks this room is his. Every time the door is open he's in here, whether there is a paying guest in the room or not!"

"Was he here six years ago?" asked Marguerite, staring at him.

"Oh, yes, Jericho has been here ten years," returned Mrs. Hammond bitterly. "I call him Jericho because that's where I'm always wishing he was—at Jericho!"

Jericho looked unperturbed, his tail giving a casual

twitch of acknowledgment to this triple mention of his name.

"I did manage to keep him out that night, though, miss, if that's what's worrying you. I wouldn't have had your mother bothered by such a thing—but it took some doing, I can tell you."

"I'm sure it did," returned Marguerite, smiling and scratching Jericho behind the ears. "It wouldn't have mattered, though. Mama loved animals. She wouldn't have minded."

"There's something else, miss," said Mrs. Hammond hesitantly. "I thought about it last night after we talked."

Marguerite waited expectantly while Jericho, the only one in the room who felt entirely comfortable, watched them both with a steady gaze.

"I stayed with your mother after she was taken so bad," she said slowly, twisting her starched white apron. "And at the last, she seemed to rally just a little, like she was trying to say something."

"What was it?" asked Marguerite eagerly. "What did she say, Mrs. Hammond?"

The lady shook her head, setting the ribbons on her cap fluttering. "I couldn't say for sure, miss, but it sounded like 'Onjeleek.' "

Marguerite's face fell. "Angelique. That was her name. Did she say anything else?"

Mrs. Hammond shook her head again, more vigorously this time, creating a veritable windstorm of ribbons. "I think she was trying, miss, but she fell back on her pillow and it was over."

Marguerite stared at the pillow behind Jericho and blinked back the tears. She was glad the cat was there, though. He gave a simple, homely touch to something that would have otherwise seemed too grim to bear. She thanked Mrs. Hammond again and slipped back down the stairs to join the others in the chaise. Although Celia looked at her with an inquiring glance, she did not give voice to her questions, and Sir Richard did not dignify her late arrival with an acknowledgment.

The rest of their journey was without incident. Their stop that night was at another comfortable posting house—or it was at least as comfortable as posting houses could be—and it was unremarkable in any way. Celia was chiefly occupied the whole of the trip with Nipper's well-being, and, when not concerned with that, she was lulled gently to sleep by the motion of the carriage.

At one point in the trip, Sir Richard looked back at them and Celia was again sleeping peacefully, a wing of silver hair that had escaped her bonnet swinging next to eyelashes that were as dark as Marguerite's. Not many young women showed to advantage while sleeping, reflected her sister complacently, but Celia was a decided exception.

Sir Richard appeared to agree with her, saying simply, "Most of the women I know would give their very souls to look like that, yet she is not even aware of it. I should hate to see her change." And he turned back to the book that he had been reading.

Rather astonished by his reaction, Marguerite opened *Sense and Sensibility* again. If a man as difficult to impress as Sir Richard Norwood was so struck by Celia, she would surely have her selection of husbands. It appeared that their difficult times were behind them.

She was, however, less inclined to feel that way after they were installed at Norwood House in London. Although she was eager to see everything as they entered the city, the noise and bustle of the traffic struck her almost like a physical blow. For one who had lived always in a rural atmosphere, the assault upon the senses was at first almost too much to bear. She had expected this, though, and felt that she would soon adjust. Celia, her eyes wide and frightened as she whispered soothing words to Nipper, who was inclined to object to all of the noise and bouncing about, was quite another matter. Marguerite could not give her full attention to the view during the rest of their drive through London, for she was busily applying herself to lifting her sister's spirits, pointing out such comforting sights as the entrance to the pleasures of Hyde Park and a gingerbread man on the corner, dispensing his wares.

They had no fault to find with their reception at Norwood House: the butler and two elegantly attired footmen swept down the steps of the mansion to usher them in, and they were shown to their chambers where they were immediately waited upon by maids bearing tea trays and large receptacles of hot water. There was ample time, they were informed, for them to rest before dinner, and if they were too worn by their journey to come down for dinner, it would be brought to them.

Celia, exhausted by the excitement, had taken to her bed as soon as she had inspected her chamber and installed Nipper in the most protected place, and Marguerite had stayed with her long enough to be certain that she was indeed asleep. Marguerite was too excited to wish to remain in her room; her desire was to go out and look round the city immediately. She had already recovered from the first shock of the bustle of the city, and she had caught only the most tantalizing glimpses as they had arrived. She knew, however, that a young lady should not walk alone on the streets of London, so she contented herself with looking out her window to the street below as she sipped her tea.

The time passed slowly for her, though, and she paced about the room for a while before forcing herself to enjoy the unheard-of luxury of a fire in her own chamber, settling herself quietly before it and reading *Sense and Sensibility*. She thought of going downstairs, but the maid had told her that they would be called when dinner was served, and she was reluctant to wander about, having not yet met Lady Norwood.

The afternoon finally ended and she awakened Celia in ample time for her to prepare for dinner. As usual, she gave herself the pleasure of dressing Celia's hair. As she glanced into the glass, Marguerite smiled at her handiwork. Celia, attired in cerulean blue, looked as delightful as she always did, even though she had insisted upon having her hair dressed with black ribbons and wearing a rather elderly black shawl that had belonged to Mama. Marguerite had objected to her wearing black, but Celia, who was still feeling guilty about putting off her mourning, had been unusually firm.

Marguerite herself had felt no such guilt, and, although she was not a breathtaking vision like Celia, she was not displeased with the picture she presented. Her gown, too, had been fashioned from one of Mama's, a silk the color of a fine claret wine, and her dark curls were caught up with a pair of golden combs that she had found in Mama's trunk. The finishing touch was Mama's wedding ring, a single perfect pearl in a quaint gold filigree setting. Her mother had often remarked—but not in front of Papa, of course, who disapproved heartily of such vanity—that one day the ring, along with the necklace and earrings that matched it, would be hers. She had never seen the necklace and earrings, but she had thought when she found the trunk that perhaps Mama had put them away there to keep them out of Papa's sight. Her mother had been permitted to wear the ring only because it had served as their wedding ring. He frequently mentioned, however, that it should be sold and the money given to the poor, saying that a plain gold band would do well enough for a wedding ring. He never did so, however, since the ring had been her mother's before their marriage. Papa was stern, but he was a just man. To her disappointment, Marguerite had not discovered them in the trunk nor among any other of her mother's things and had given them up for lost. Tonight, however, she wore the ring with pride.

The girls went down to dinner with some trepidation. Marguerite did not expect to meet Lady Norwood at dinner, thinking that perhaps she and Celia would be escorted to her chamber afterwards. She had assumed that illness would still have her confined to her bed.

As they entered the drawing room, however, a languid beauty in a brocade gown the color of green apples raised her lorgnette to survey them. Startled, the young ladies paused for a moment and allowed themselves to be studied. Then the vision spoke. "So you are dear Angelique's girls. How delightful to see you at last."

Marguerite noted quickly that she did not sound particularly delighted; instead, she sounded quite bored. Then she shook herself mentally, giving herself a severe reminder that the lady had suffered a long illness and could not be expected to sound enthusiastic about anything.

Lady Norwood, dropping the lorgnette that hung on a ribbon round her neck, raised a lace-mittened hand to each of them in turn, exerting the least possible effort in doing so. "Which of you is which, my dears? Do come closer so that I may see you clearly."

"I am Marguerite, Lady Norwood, and this is my sister Celia." Together they approached the sofa upon which Lady Norwood was gracefully reclining. "We are delighted to meet you at last. It is very kind of you to invite us to visit, particularly when you have not been well."

"I am seldom in good health, my dear. I have a very fragile constitution, you see, and so I must be cautious," sighed Lady Norwood, leaning back and closing her eyes for a moment. "I avoid fatigue whenever possible."

"You may be assured of that," commented Sir Richard dryly. "Lady Norwood does *not* fatigue herself in any manner whatsoever."

Marguerite blinked at the sound of his voice, for she

had not noticed him standing in a corner of the room, surveying the scene before him. Lady Norwood shot a venomous glance in his direction but did not dignify his comment with a response, turning back to the young ladies instead.

"And so you are my namesake," she said to Marguerite, studying her closely. "We do not resemble one another, of course, but I shall be interested to see if perhaps we are alike in character. That sometimes happens, you know, between namesakes."

"Then God help us all," murmured Sir Richard in a low voice that was just audible to the ladies.

Again there was a flash of fire from Lady Norwood's pale blue eyes, but again she made no remark to the gentleman. Marguerite was struck by that interchange, as she had been by the first, but she could not give it her whole attention. Standing close to Lady Norwood as she was now, Marguerite could see that she was wearing the necklace and earrings that matched Mama's ring. Celia noticed it, too, and glanced quickly at her sister. Lady Norwood, although intent now upon studying Celia, did not appear to be aware of anything unusual.

"My dear child," she said softly, extending a mittened hand to draw Celia closer to her, "how very much you look like Angelique. Were you just a trifle shorter, I should almost believe that my dear friend were with me again. Come and kiss me, my dear."

And Celia, touched by the reference to her mother, leaned over and gently kissed the ivory cheek that Lady Norwood indicated to her. "We were so sorry to hear of your illness, Lady Norwood. I hope that you will allow us to be of some help to you," she said softly.

"How very dear you are!" exclaimed Lady Norwood. "I shall look upon you as the daughters I was never blessed with. How delighted with you Philippe will be!"

Seeing that Marguerite and Celia looked puzzled, Lady

Norwood flushed and once again threw an angry glance in Sir Richard's direction. "How very like you, Richard, to have spent all of this time with them and not to have mentioned your brother!"

Turning back to Celia, she said in a much more affable tone, "Philippe is my son, you see. He will be joining us in Bath, and he will be quite overcome to see that he now has sisters to look after."

"I should imagine that 'overcome' is precisely what he will be," contributed Sir Richard, picking up a vase from the mantel and eyeing it idly.

"You must not listen to Richard," said Lady Norwood in a brittle voice. "He has been bad-tempered from the time he was a child. It comes of being too much indulged by his father."

Sir Richard glanced at her sharply, but she ignored him and turned the conversation away from him, saying to Celia, "I do hope that you will help me in to dinner, my dear. As you can see, I cannot depend upon Richard to lend me his support, even though he should be the one escorting me."

Celia gave Sir Richard an apologetic glance and allowed Lady Norwood, rising slowly from her couch, to lean upon her as they made their way slowly into the dining room. Sir Richard offered his arm to Marguerite with an ironic glance, saying, "Are you surprised, Miss Standish, to see what a happy little family we are? Do you think you will enjoy your visit as much as you had expected?"

Marguerite forced herself to smile pleasantly, hoping that he would find it annoying. "I had done you an injustice, Sir Richard," she replied sweetly. "I do hope that you will accept my apology."

He looked down at her, clearly surprised by her words. "And what injustice have you done me, Miss Standish?" he inquired.

"I had thought, sir, that you had singled me out to be

the object of your bad manners and short temper. I see tonight, however, that you treat others in the same manner—you are quite egalitarian. One might almost think you were French."

To her irritation, he did not respond to her sally at all, nor did his expression alter, so she added sharply, "Being a lady does not seem to make any difference in the manner of treatment one receives at your hands. It appears that my sister is the only one to whom you show the slightest consideration."

Here his expression did change, and his voice grew almost gentle. "Miss Celia? Yes, Miss Celia is quite another matter from you and my lovely stepmother, Miss Standish. Surely you yourself can distinguish the difference."

His comment threw Marguerite completely off course. She was angered by his cavalier treatment of herself and Lady Norwood and pleased by his ability to value Celia—but bothered by it, too. She had no desire for Sir Richard to grow too interested in her gentle sister. She had in mind a far different kind of man for Celia. Certainly the forbidding gentleman next to her would bring no happiness to the lady he wedded.

Being in such a novel situation at first made Marguerite ill at ease, for the number of footmen stationed about the impressive room seemed out of all proportion to the four of them seated at the table. Counting the butler, there were five servants present in the room. That should just about take care of us, she thought to herself. One to cut the food for each of us, and one to serve the new courses. Mrs. Ruscombe's manor was well staffed, but Marguerite had never felt that she was tripping over a servant every time she turned around. She wondered who was responsible for the excessive display of servants at Norwood House.

She supposed that it must be Lady Norwood, for this must surely be her house, and yet Sir Richard was—apparently—the heir, and so perhaps Lady Norwood was here as a guest in her position as dowager, and the extravagant display of wealth was Sir Richard's. She found herself wanting to attribute it wholly to him because he annoyed her, and she would like to think that ostentation was simply one more of his many shortcomings. However, aside from the fact that she had invited them here, Marguerite really had no reason to take the part of Lady Norwood either. She could note no resemblance between that lady and Mama or Celia, either in face or in manner.

It was not until the second course that she began to focus on what was going on at the table; the conversation had been only sporadic, and it was as she being served the roast lamb and mint sauce that Lady Norwood's question brought her back to reality.

"Why, Marguerite, my child, just look at the ring you are wearing! It is the one that belongs to my set, the one your dear mother used as her wedding ring. Had you not noticed my necklace and earrings?"

"Indeed I had, Lady Norwood," Marguerite stammered, caught completely off guard by her question. "I am afraid, though, that I don't understand."

Lady Norwood raised her perfectly arched eyebrows. "What is it that you don't understand, Marguerite?"

"I knew that this was Mama's wedding ring, of course, but—" Marguerite began slowly.

"But she hadn't told you the story of how that came to be!" exclaimed Lady Norwood, laughing lightly. "I suppose she felt it might have embarrassed your father, for, you see, he came to church that morning without a ring at all. It had flown completely out of his mind. There were only four of us, your mother and father and *my* Richard and I."

Here she threw a glance at Sir Richard to see if he had noticed her emphasis. If he had, he gave no sign of it, and she continued. "So, it seemed to be up to me. I was wearing that set and I took off the ring and handed it to your father—and I told them later that I wanted them to keep it. It was good luck for both of us. Richard and I were married just three days later."

"I see," murmured Marguerite—although she did not see at all. It was difficult to imagine Papa ever being at a loss or being unprepared for such a moment as a wedding, even though it had been just a brief, informal ceremony. And Mama had certainly never told her this story.

Celia, too, was looking puzzled. "But I had always thought that the set belonged to Mama. Marguerite, did she not tell you that the set would one day belong to you?"

Before she could make an embarrassed reply to her sister's question, Lady Norwood had risen impulsively from her place and stepped over to Marguerite. Undoing the clasp of the necklace, she slipped it around her young guest's throat and stepped back to view her work.

"Charming!" she proclaimed, admiring her handiwork. "I shall send Tolliver to you with the earrings tonight. They will look quite delightful on you, my dear, and there is no one that I would prefer to see wearing them more than Angelique's daughter."

"I can't accept them, Lady Norwood," protested Marguerite, mired deep in embarrassment now. "I beg your pardon for making you feel that you should do this for me."

"Nonsense!" exclaimed Lady Norwood. "I would not do this if I didn't wish to." She studied her young guest for a moment. "We shall look delightful together, you and I, your dark hair contrasting so well with my golden hair. You must sit close to me when we have guests and act as a foil for me."

She turned to Celia, who was listening to her plan in amazement. "And you, my dear, shall sit on the other side of Marguerite, and we shall be a most remarkable picture of beauty. I daresay someone will compose verses about us."

Celia looked even more startled, and Sir Richard's brief laugh was drier than ever. "Don't worry, Miss Celia," he told her, ignoring the others. "I would not expect a sudden onslaught of poets tomorrow morning. It will take Lady Norwood a little time to arrange her admiring audience, and I fear that she will have to wait until you are settled in Bath. And so, you see, you have a reprieve."

Celia smiled uncertainly, still not sure precisely what anyone was talking about. Lady Norwood rose from her place, announcing in an arctic tone that it was time that the ladies adjourned to the drawing room and left Sir Richard to the pleasure of his own company.

"No doubt, sir, you will find that much more elevating," she announced, sweeping grandly from the room.

Celia hurried in her wake, but Marguerite, having dropped her handkerchief, was less quick in making her exit. Sir Richard raised his glass to her in a toast, his expression sardonic.

"Congratulations, Miss Standish. You are already doing very well for yourself, are you not?"

Marguerite stared at him, puzzled, but did not reply.

"I refer to the necklace," he explained patiently, taking a sip from the glass. "And, of course, to the earrings that Tolliver will duly deliver tonight."

Marguerite's cheeks flamed and she glanced at the four footmen ranged impassively round the room. "You amaze me, Sir Richard," she said in a low voice. "You, as I understand it, are supposed to be a gentleman—and yet you insult me—and do so in front of others."

Sir Richard glanced at the nearest footman, whose expression had not altered by the blink of an eye. "Oh, I wouldn't worry unduly about them, Miss Standish—servants are trained never to see or hear anything. And, as for insulting you, I certainly was not doing so. I was complimenting your skills. You set out to do well for yourself in this venture, and you have begun in the most promising manner. I salute you!"

Seeing that it was impossible to speak reasonably with him, Marguerite turned and marched from the room, her head high. Their visit to Lady Norwood was beginning to take on a most unpleasant aspect. She wondered whether Lady Norwood held the same view of her that her stepson did. If so, their visit, even if it were to end tomorrow, would seem long indeed. Her belief that her mother and Lady Norwood were somehow related seemed a distant and foolish dream.

Marguerite entered the drawing room with the hope that the evening would soon be over, but she could see at once that Lady Norwood was aching to unburden herself.

"You see what I must contend with," she said plaintively, leaning back on the sofa and resting her head on her hand. "It absolutely exhausts me to have these confrontations with Richard. He shows no consideration for my fragile health."

Marguerite was not particularly impressed with her fragility, feeling that it came and went at will, but on the subject of confrontations with her unpleasant stepson, Lady Norwood had all of her sympathy. However, since she was still far too angry to be able to say so, it was fortunate that Celia was prepared to respond.

"I daresay that he simply does not think of it," she explained gently. "Gentlemen are often in such vigorous health that they don't realize what it is like for someone with a delicate constitution."

Lady Norwood looked distinctly pleased with her. "How very observant of you, my dear. Very often young people are so hearty themselves that they forget that not everyone enjoys the same rude health. Not," she added as an afterthought, "that I am no longer young myself, but at least I have had time to grow more thoughtful and observant."

At least twenty years, thought Marguerite to herself,

growing less impressed by her hostess with every word
that she uttered. Having observed Lady Norwood during
the course of the evening, she had decided that she was
not an invalid at all; she simply used illness as a convenient weapon to aid her in having her own way. She was
surprised that Sir Richard endured it at all, having formed
an accurate opinion of that gentleman's lack of tolerance.

It was with profound gratitude that Marguerite made
her way to her chamber that evening. She refused the assistance of a maid to prepare for bed, preferring to be
alone as she always was, except for slipping across the
corridor to say good night to Celia and Nipper and to be
certain that all was well with them.

Before she retired, however, there was another knock at
the door, and she opened it to find a tall, unsmiling female
with a face rather like a hatchet.

"Miss Standish?" the specter demanded sharply.

Marguerite nodded.

"I was told to bring you these," said the specter, shov-
ing a small velvet box toward Marguerite. "Although I'm
sure that I don't know *why* I was told to do so, nor for
that matter why you are here, miss," she added with a
sniff. Without another word, she turned and walked away.

Marguerite closed the door and opened the box slowly.
Lady Norwood had been as good as her word. In the box
lay the dainty earrings that she had been wearing at dinner. How very kind of her it was to send them, Marguerite
reflected, wondering how she had come to believe that the
set belonged to Mama. It was most curious.

Still, it was delightful to have them, and she held them
up to her ears and admired them in the glass. And although Lady Norwood had given them graciously, it appeared that Tolliver, her maid, did not view the gift in the
same light. She, no doubt, would have agreed wholeheart-
edly with Sir Richard. Thinking of that, Marguerite sank

down on the edge of her bed, the earrings still in her hand and the pleasure gone from the gift.

Although Sir Richard clearly held her in low esteem and suspected her motives for coming to Norwood House, she still could not imagine that he would have written the anonymous note. Tolliver, however, was another matter. It was evident that Tolliver did not care for her either—could she perhaps be the author of the note?

In the excitement of the journey and the arrival, she had put aside all thought of that unpleasant letter, but now it all came back sharply. Was there, she wondered, any reason to fear Tolliver's dislike, or was it simply the natural jealousy of a devoted servant for someone in whom her mistress appeared to be interested? Although the matter was of importance to Marguerite, she found that she could not keep her attention focused upon it, and she finally drifted away to sleep.

Six

Greatly to her relief, Marguerite discovered that she and Celia would breakfast alone the following morning, for Lady Norwood would have her chocolate in her room and Sir Richard had arisen much earlier to go riding. Her pleasure was short-lived, however, for their host, in smooth buckskin trousers and an impeccably cut riding coat, joined them before they had finished dining. The picture of elegance even after riding, she thought to herself, profoundly annoyed.

He greeted them abruptly and then seated himself carelessly next to Celia, crossing his legs and absently tapping the toe of highly polished boot with his riding crop, appearing to fall into a temporary brown study. It was Marguerite's devout hope that he remain preoccupied, for she certainly had no desire to speak to him. Her hope was soon dashed, however.

"And so, ladies, what are your plans for today?" he inquired, suddenly rousing himself. He addressed them both, but looked across the table at Marguerite. "Shopping? Morning calls? Shall you be arranging the pose that my dear stepmother spoke of so fondly last night?"

When there was no immediate response from the young ladies—or, more properly, from Marguerite, to whom he appeared to be addressing these barbs—he added, "And it is a thousand pities, I know, that we are leaving for Bath tomorrow, so that there will not be time for my stepmother to bring her powers of persuasion to bear on Lady Sefton to acquire vouchers to Almack's for you."

Marguerite hoped that she did not look as ill as she suddenly felt. Almack's! She knew from her reading and from listening to Mrs. Ruscombe that this was the vital entrée into society for any young lady, particularly one new to the London scene. To be accepted at Almack's was to be accepted by the *ton*. She had hoped that Celia would have the opportunity to make her appearance there, but it was clear that this was not to be. She had not realized that their removal to Bath would be so immediate.

Mustering her forces, Marguerite faced her tormentor with a cool composure. "I believe that you are aware that we shall be doing none of those things, Sir Richard. As I have made clear to you, we cannot afford shopping sprees, and, as you also know quite well, we are acquainted with no one else in London save you and Lady Norwood, so we are dependent entirely upon you to determine any outings that we may take. It is my understanding that a well-bred young lady does not even take a walk around the square unless she is accompanied by a servant or a chaperone. Since we have neither, we apparently have no freedom of movement at all."

She paused for a tenth of a second to draw a breath, then forced herself to smile at him pleasantly and add, "So, as you must know, Sir Richard, your questions are idle ones, since we must in everything rely upon your generosity."

It had galled her to say these things, although she had been thinking them and regretting the degree to which someone else now controlled their lives, but she felt a sharp rise of triumph when she saw that her Parthian shot had struck home, for Sir Richard was looking shamefaced. She was surprised—but gratified—that he was at all vulnerable to such remarks.

His state was not aided by Celia, who interjected hurriedly, "And we would not wish to do any of those things, of course, unless we were certain that Lady Norwood had no need of us. After all, she is our hostess and we should attend to her comfort before seeking pleasure for ourselves."

Marguerite reflected, not for the first time, that Papa's teachings had taken far too great a hold on Celia's mind. She was inclined to suffer guilt anytime that she was enjoying herself, particularly if she felt that someone else was unhappy. Her sincerity, however, was clear, and Sir Richard held up his hands in surrender.

"Forgive me, ladies, for my boorish behavior. I have deserved it all, I realize. What would you have of me by way of apology? A drive round the city? You saw precious little of it as we came in yesterday."

Celia looked dubious, remembering the clamor of the streets, but Marguerite was enthusiastic. "Yes, we should like it above all things, Sir Richard." She was perfectly willing to set her pride aside and go out with this arrogant man if it meant that she got to see London. He did at least owe them that much. And, for the moment at least, she felt that he might be more gentlemanly, having had his ill-mannered behavior so sharply brought home to him.

And that appeared to be the case, for no one could have been more charming a host than was Sir Richard for the next few hours. Marguerite had to remind herself that this was the same man who had accused her of feathering her own nest the evening before. She felt rather pleased with herself for causing such an about-face in a man so accustomed to having his own way.

In deference to their comfort and pleasure, he had Lady Norwood's old-fashioned landau brought around. It was not until she was better acquainted with Sir Richard that Marguerite realized what a sacrifice it was for him to take them driving in such a dowdy vehicle when he was known for his far more dashing curricle and four. She did notice a few looks of amazement on their drive through Hyde Park later that afternoon, but she ascribed them to the sight of Sir Richard with such a vision as Celia beside him.

He devoted himself entirely to being an entertaining guide, pointing out the sights to them, from the elegant shops on Bond Street to St. Paul's Cathedral. When he discovered that Marguerite was eager to visit Lackington's, he dutifully stopped there and she was permitted to browse through the books to her heart's content.

"Please allow me to purchase one for you, Miss Standish," he said pleasantly, seeing the pleasure she took in them.

Coloring, she shook her head, remembering only too vividly the scene from last night. Checking to see that Celia was safely out of earshot, she said in a low voice, "I am not entirely penniless, Sir Richard, and you would doubtless view my acceptance of your offer as another indication of my greed. I shall do very well on my own, thank you."

Sir Richard, his own color heightened at her reproach, bowed stiffly. "As you wish, ma'am." He moved away to join her sister.

Her pleasure in their outing had vanished with the memory of his words, reminding her sharply of her mistreatment at his hands. As they returned to the landau, it seemed to her that the color had been drained from the day, but she forced herself to smile and be agreeable so that Celia's afternoon would not be spoiled.

When they were on their way home, Sir Richard asked what Celia had enjoyed most about the day. She smiled. "The park," she replied simply. "It made me think of home," she added in explanation, looking at the shops, elegant expanses of stone and plaster and glass, that lined the street on either side. "I miss seeing green all about me."

"Then you will enjoy Bath more than London, I believe, Miss Celia," replied Sir Richard. "The house where you

will be there offers a view of green meadows and hills—
and I shall assuredly take you to Sydney Gardens where
you may drink your fill of nature."

"You are very kind, Sir Richard," Celia replied softly,
her eyes wide with gratitude. She was not accustomed to
having anyone except Marguerite attend to her desires.

Her sister was torn by this interchange. Although she
was pleased to see that he was being kind to Celia, she
was wary, too. Why would he be so kind unless he was
developing an interest in her? He had not shown himself
to be a kindly man by nature; therefore, she must suspect
that there was some other motive for his actions. She
promised herself that she would watch the situation carefully. Celia could not fall prey to such a man as this.

When they reached Norwood House, they saw that
preparations for the next day's journey were already in
motion. To their amazement, the young ladies learned that
two carts loaded with the household goods deemed necessary for their stay, another loaded with luggage, and a
large, old-fashioned berlin carrying the butler, the cook,
two maids, and two footmen had already departed for Bath
to prepare the house for Lady Norwood's arrival.

"How exhausting it will be," sighed that lady, once
again reclining on a sofa in the drawing room. "My vinaigrette, Tolliver," she added, extending her hand. "I feel
quite faint just thinking of it."

Tolliver ministered to her silently, casting a grim look
at Marguerite and Celia, quite as though they were responsible for Lady Norwood's condition. Sir Richard had
discreetly vanished at the mention of the vinaigrette.

"I do hope that *you* had a pleasant day," said their hostess in a voice barely removed from a moan. "I am sorry
that I was not able to take you about myself, but, as you
can see, it was quite beyond me."

Celia assured her that they had not expected her to do
any such thing and, glancing back toward the trunks and

bandboxes still waiting in the foyer, added guiltily that they would have stayed to help Lady Norwood had they realized the magnitude of her undertaking.

"It was indeed depleting, dear child," said Lady Norwood, holding the vinaigrette to her nose again. "I am sure, however, that the waters will restore me. Then, perhaps, I will be spared such fearful headaches as the one I have just now."

Marguerite murmured something sympathetic, but her heart was not in it. She was quite certain that their hostess had had no hand at all in the preparations and was merely fond of playing the martyr. She even had doubts about the severity of the headache just mentioned. Still, she reminded herself sharply that they were guests and should be properly grateful to the person responsible for their invitation.

"I am so sorry to be dragging you away from London, my dears, when you have only just arrived," continued their hostess, "but I simply am not equal to any sort of regular social life just yet, and my doctor recommended the stay at Bath. I'm afraid, though, that it will be fearfully dull for the two of you."

Marguerite feared much the same thing, but Celia hastened to assure her that they were prepared to be of service to Lady Norwood and that their own entertainment was not a matter of consequence. Marguerite, who saw every day that slipped by as a day that took them farther from her goal for Celia and closer to disaster, tried to echo her sister's sentiments, but her voice was hollow.

Fortunately, Lady Norwood did not appear to notice this, being fully occupied by Celia's ministrations. She had dabbed a bit of the scented vinegar onto a small handkerchief and was bathing Lady Norwood's temples with it.

You dear child," she murmured, "how restful you are, how very soothing. Tolliver, if your touch were only this gentle, my headache might have dissipated long ago."

Tolliver did not, of course, reply, and Marguerite glanced at her, standing like a dark guardian angel behind her mistress. She was startled by the look of fierce hatred burning in the maid's eyes. She seemed unaware of Marguerite, but she was following Celia's every move.

Celia continued her attendance on Lady Norwood for another few minutes until Tolliver reminded her gruffly that it was time for her to change for dinner. Smiling at Celia, Lady Norwood raised a hand to pat the girl's cheek lovingly.

"So very like my dear friend," she murmured. "Always kind, always thinking of others."

Marguerite was grateful to see them leave, and found herself wondering about Tolliver. That she was possessive of her mistress and jealous of her prerogative to wait upon her was obvious. Marguerite reflected that it would be as well if they kept a respectable distance from Lady Norwood, but she was certain that she would never be able to convince Celia of that.

Marguerite dressed for dinner in the second of her two suitable gowns, an elderly dark silk of her own, slightly refurbished by the knotted ribbons of old gold that she had used to retrim it.

"You look lovely, Marguerite," said Celia as she came in to wait for her. "You are going to wear the necklace that Lady Norwood gave you, aren't you? It would look very well with that gown, and it would be a compliment to her as well."

Marguerite thought of what Sir Richard's expression would be when he saw the necklace and almost shook her head, but then she was angry with herself for feeling guilt when she had no reason to do so. Angry with him for being so busy about other people's affairs, she took the necklace from its box and allowed Celia to fasten it about her neck.

"I shall wear the earrings, too," she announced firmly,

quite as though Celia had been arguing against doing any such thing.

"Well, of course you should do so," Celia agreed, a little startled by her tone. "It is the first time that you have ever worn the complete set." She smiled down at Marguerite. "Mama would be so pleased. She always intended that you have these."

Marguerite's own pleasure faded a little with her words. "I still have no idea what was meant by all of this," she said slowly, fingering the necklace. "I remember Mama saying that, too, and yet—I suppose that perhaps Lady Norwood had promised the rest of the set to her, and she died before she received it."

Celia nodded eagerly. "I hadn't thought of that. Naturally Mama did not expect to die so young. She must have thought that there would be more than enough time, for very likely she wouldn't have given them to you until you were at least seventeen."

Satisfied by this explanation, the two of them went downstairs together, Marguerite striking in her old dark gown and gold filigree and pearls, Celia as angelic as usual in a white slip bound with a robe of cerulean blue. The picture they made as they paused together at the entrance of the drawing room was the more striking because they were entirely unaware of it.

"I don't know, Marguerite, that you would make a good third in that portrait," said Sir Richard to his stepmother in a low voice, his eyes mocking. "Just see how they look together—dawn and dusk. What would you be, my dear stepmama? Late afternoon?"

And he eased away from her to the young ladies at the door before she could retort.

"You must forgive us for dining *en famille* again, ladies," he said, bowing to them. "I know that it must be tiresome to have only us at the table again tonight. It may be that in Bath there will be more to entertain you."

Before Celia could disclaim any such desire, Lady Norwood spoke, her tone frosty. "I believe that they—unlike
you, my *most* considerate son—are aware that my health
forbids it. And I have explained to them that we will not
be entertaining on a grand scale in Bath, either."

"How very ungenerous of you, Marguerite," he countered. "Does this mean that you will do nothing save take
the waters and come directly home to bed? No concerts,
no balls at the Assembly Rooms, no breakfasts, no plays?
I shall know, if I hear that this is the case, that you are
indeed at death's door."

"You are the most unnatural son!" she flared, shaken
for the moment from her languid pose. "However you
could be so different from your father I cannot imagine!"

His response was distant and unmistakably cold. "I am
not your son, madam. I would have thought that we had
established that some time ago. As for being different
from my father, I suppose I am. Unlike him, I could see
through you from the beginning."

Before anyone else could say anything to break the ten-
sion, he turned to Celia and offered her his arm. "Shall
we go in to dinner, Miss Celia?" he inquired in quite a
different tone. "I promise that I shall not snap your nose
off, so don't be afraid."

Celia colored as she took his arm. "Indeed, I'm not at
all afraid of you, Sir Richard. You have been too kind to
me for me to fear you."

As they left the room, Marguerite could hear her sister
laughing and telling him of Nipper's latest exploits when
she let him out of his cage to explore his new room. She
turned reluctantly back to Lady Norwood, who was still
seething on the sofa.

"How he dares to insult me in my own home, I fail to
understand! I have no difficulty in seeing why his father
wished to cast him off! I wish that he had not died before
doing so!"

Marguerite stared at her, horrified. She had no desire to be a part of any household so filled with ill feeling, nor to be the recipient of such bitter confidences. She thought of Tolliver glaring at Celia that afternoon and of Lady Norwood and Sir Richard coming to verbal fisticuffs just now. Was there no peace at all in this household?

Lady Norwood, recovering a semblance of her composure, held up her hand to Marguerite. "It appears that we must make do with one another, Marguerite. I shall try not to lean upon you too much, my dear."

Dinner passed more smoothly than either of the sisters had expected that it would. Both of the offenders appeared to regret their earlier outburst and, although it could not be said that their relations were amicable, they were at least able to stay at the table without insulting one another. The talk turned to the travel arrangements for tomorrow, and the young ladies learned that they would again be traveling with Sir Richard in his chaise, while Tolliver and Lady Norwood occupied hers.

"I must lie down for the course of the journey, you see," explained Lady Norwood apologetically, "otherwise I would insist upon taking you with me. Indeed," she continued thoughtfully, her eye upon Celia, "I do think that there would be room for you, my dear—and it would do me so much good to have you with me."

At your beck and call, you mean, thought Marguerite, her heart sinking. Before she could say anything, however, Sir Richard intervened.

"I am afraid that Miss Celia is not traveling alone, Marguerite," he said smoothly, accepting a serving of boiled capon and oysters.

"Well, of course I am aware that she is traveling with her sister, Richard," she replied sharply. "I am not in my dotage, you know."

"Indeed not, Marguerite. But I was not referring to her sister but to—to Nipper."

"Nipper?" inquired Lady Norwood, mystified. "Who is Nipper?"

"A canary," returned Sir Richard before either of the sisters could respond. "A canary that requires considerable attention and space. I fear that you would not have enough space for Miss Celia *and* Nipper."

"Well, that is no problem. Nipper can remain with you, Celia with me." Lady Norwood, once she had hold of an idea, released it only reluctantly.

Sir Richard shook his head. "I fear that I could not permit it, ma'am," he said gravely.

His stepmother bristled. "How dare you say that you will not permit it, Richard?" she demanded. "By what right do you say that to me?"

For the first time since the conversation had begun, he looked at her directly, and his eyes were brooding. "You know quite well by what right I speak, madam—but we will not go into that now. Suffice it to say that I have the right of a gentleman to say it. Miss Standish cannot travel alone from here to Bath in a closed carriage with a man not her relative. Her sister must be with her."

"What fustian!" exclaimed Lady Norwood. "As though anyone attended to such antiquated notions anymore!"

"You know quite well that such notions *are* attended to, however, and we will also honor them. Miss Standish is our guest and we will not do anything to sully her reputation."

Lady Norwood looked inclined to be mulish, but when she again met Sir Richard's gaze, her own gave way first.

"Very well," she exclaimed pettishly, raising one elegant shoulder in a shrug. "It really does not matter greatly to me at any rate."

"We are all relieved to hear your gracious acceptance of the situation, ma'am," returned Sir Richard gravely, his eyes still fixed on his stepmother. Marguerite noticed that as his gaze did not drop, the lady grew more and more

restive, until she suddenly announced that they would retire to the drawing room without dessert.

They left Sir Richard alone in the dining room, and he
did not join them for coffee after his port. Marguerite was
grateful, for she had no desire to witness any more ex-
changes between the two of them this evening. She had
a great deal to think about, however, and she was deeply
grateful that he had rescued Celia from his stepmother's
clutches. She had no desire to see Celia become a sort of
household slave for Lady Norwood. Nor, it appeared, did
Sir Richard. She did not for a moment believe that he
gave a fig for her reputation—that argument had served
only to extract Celia from a difficult situation.

"It is no wonder that his father sent him away," shuddered Lady Norwood in the privacy of the drawing room.
"He has a most *violent* temper—you have not really seen
it yet. Why I suspect that he is capable of the most terrible
of deeds when he is in one of his black rages!"

"Oh, surely not, Lady Norwood!" exclaimed Celia, unwilling to let him be abused even by her hostess. "He
has been kindness itself in his treatment of us."

Marguerite reflected that she would not be saying so if
she had seen his behavior over the necklace, but she held
her peace.

"Then you had best be very careful, my dear," replied
Lady Norwood gravely. "He must have a reason for behaving in what for him is a most unnatural manner." She
shuddered again. "I am more than grateful that he will
not stay long in Bath."

"Will he return to London?" asked Marguerite curiously, ready to be quite as grateful as Lady Norwood if
he were leaving them.

She shook her head. "He will be going back again to
Greenwood Park. He never stays away from there any
longer than he can help. I can't imagine why he so enjoys
being buried in the country, but I am grateful for it be-

cause he never stays with us long. Even when he is in London, he does not stay at Norwood House. He keeps a very different sort of company."

She paused a moment and stared at the dark-eyed man in the portrait above the fireplace. "I sometimes wonder if Richard cared at all about his father's death. He was so eager to have Greenwood Park that I think there would have been no price too high to pay."

Marguerite and Celia made their escape from the drawing room as soon as they were able, pleading the strain of the coming trip, Celia encouraging Lady Norwood to go early to bed herself to prepare for the day.

"How distraught she is," said Celia in a low voice once they were in the privacy of her chamber. "I know that she cannot mean the things she says of Sir Richard. I daresay that her illness has made her subject to unpleasant fancies."

Marguerite murmured a reply, not willing to share her troubling thoughts with Celia. She had caught a glimpse of great bitterness today and it had frightened her. She wondered how deep the roots of it ran and could only hope that Sir Richard would depart for his estate as soon as he escorted them safely to Bath. Surely then living would regain a more even tenor.

Seven

The journey to Bath was much more pleasant than the young ladies had anticipated, for they had feared that sparring matches between Lady Norwood and Sir Richard would break out whenever they stopped. The pair in question had apparently decided to save themselves for a more private occasion, however, and all went peacefully enough. As they approached the rolling hills enfolding Bath and the winding Avon, Celia exclaimed with pleasure at the sight.

"They say that that is why the Romans first settled here," said Sir Richard lazily. "They felt at home because of the seven hills here, like the seven hills upon which Rome was built."

Marguerite, not wishing him to think that she knew nothing of such matters, remarked casually, "But they were not the first here, of course. Perhaps the waters of Bath will be as effective for Lady Norwood as they were for Prince Bladud."

Celia looked at her questioningly, and Marguerite continued for her sister's benefit—and also in order to show Sir Richard that, though she was neither as well-traveled nor as well-educated as he, she was not to be despised. "According to the legends, he was the well-loved, handsome heir of one of the kings of Britain—who lived long before the Romans came here. He developed leprosy—or so they called it—it could have been any mysterious skin disease that refused to go away. At any rate, since the king had to be perfect in body, it destroyed his hope of becoming king and he lived apart from the rest of the people, wandering in the woods, eventually becoming a swineherd.

"He came wandering along the Avon, and his pigs, which had apparently acquired the disease from their keeper, plunged into some hot springs bubbling at its edge. After wallowing about a bit and then rolling over the grass to tidy themselves up, they returned to Bladud, who was astounded—for all signs of their illness had disappeared."

"And what did he do?" demanded Celia. "Did he try it himself?"

Marguerite nodded. "It seemed the only sensible thing to do, for after all, what worked for the pigs might very well work for a man—and it did. He went directly home and presented himself to his father—and of course there was all manner of rejoicing, for he was greatly loved."

"And did he become king?" Celia inquired.

Marguerite again nodded. "In due time he took the throne, and when he did, it is said that he immediately—in 863 B.C., for the legend is quite precise—that he immediately made Bath his seat and that he gathered water from the hot springs in great stone cisterns so that other sufferers could benefit from them as he had—and as the pigs had, of course."

"I do enjoy happy endings," Celia said, heaving a sigh of relief and pleasure. "With those old legends you never know. He might very well have kept the disease and wandered about forever."

"Quite right," agreed her sister, "many of those legends are as grim—or grimmer—than life. And Bladud was father to King Lear, the model for Shakespeare's play—and you know that that is not the most joyous of tales."

Sir Richard had been listening, his head turned toward them from his position in the front seat. Celia leaned forward and tapped him, something that Marguerite noted with a lack of enthusisasm, for it was an intimacy that was almost unheard-of for one as shy as her sister.

"You can see, Sir Richard, that Marguerite is an excellent teacher," she said, smiling. "She has taught me ever since our mother died when I was eleven."

"Indeed?" returned Sir Richard, his eyebrows lifting. Marguerite did not miss the note of surprise in his voice and was annoyed that he should think her incapable of doing such a thing. Or more likely, he thought her too occupied with herself to spend such time on Celia. "I can see that you have a definite interest in ancient legends, Miss Standish. Are you as accomplished in other areas?"

"Oh, she is, Sir Richard," replied Celia—with too much enthusiasm, Marguerite thought. "She taught me to keep household accounts, to embroider and paint, to speak French, to play the piano, to dance. I learned geography—"

"That will do, Celia," laughed Marguerite, interrupting her before she could draw a breath and go on. "I am quite certain that Sir Richard is overcome."

"And so I am," he responded gravely. "If you can keep household accounts, you are both more accomplished by half than most of the ladies—or gentlemen—that I know."

Marguerite suspected him of ridiculing them—or at least her—but she could see no certain indication of it, and they were drawing close to their destination, so naturally they became occupied with watching out the windows.

The young ladies had the decided advantage of seeing Bath for the first time late on a spring afternoon, so that the golden glow of the buildings of Bath stone showed to the greatest advantage. They drove briskly past the Upper Rooms and through the Circus to the Royal Crescent, where Lady Norwood had her residence. The graceful arc of buildings, pillared and corniced, had delighted eyes far more critical than theirs. The Crescent overlooked a pleasant lawn that sloped to the lower part of the town and the river, green hills rising in the distance. It was a delightful prospect, and already Marguerite began to be reconciled to the idea of spending several weeks in Bath.

Upon arrival, they had just time to change for dinner, and Marguerite was pleasantly surprised by the atmosphere that evening. Lady Norwood appeared to be in a much more agreeable frame of mind, perhaps because her son was to arrive the next day, and even Sir Richard seemed to exert himself to be pleasant.

"There are some very pleasing walks here, Miss Standish," he informed her over lamb cutlets and cucumber. "I recall your saying that you are fond of getting out, and you will find that you and your sister will be able to take some walks that are considered quite scenic. No doubt at the Pump Room you will encounter others of a like mind and have some enjoyable excursions."

Marguerite brightened at the thought of such freedom. "We will look forward to doing just that, Sir Richard," she responded, smiling. Turning to her hostess, she inquired, "Shall we be going to the Pump Room tomorrow, Lady Norwood?"

"If I feel quite up to it after this exhausting journey, I shall go by ten o'clock," she returned, her voice failing as she thought of the early hour, for she was accustomed to sleeping until noon in London and then reading her mail and having her chocolate in bed. "I have already sent a note round to Dr. Lavenham, of course, so that he may call upon me this evening and determine if I should exert myself to such a degree."

Celia, taking her failing voice as a sign of exhaustion, leaned toward her, saying anxiously, "I'm certain that he will tell you that you must rest until you feel up to making the effort, Lady Norwood. It would be a terrible thing to set your health back by carelessness when you have made such a long journey to improve it."

"Dear child," said Lady Norwood, in the voice of one

who might expire at any moment, "you are wise beyond your years. I shall want you at my side when we do go to the Pump Room. I know that I may rely upon you to care for me properly."

"Of course you may," said Celia firmly, before Marguerite could intervene. "I shall be with you."

"Then I feel that I may be strong enough to go tomorrow morning," sighed Lady Norwood. "It is so comforting to know that there is someone I may rely upon."

How delightful a prospect, thought Marguerite. Instead of enjoying what pleasures Bath had to offer, Celia would be consigned to a diet of Oliver biscuits and mineral water and the role of maid-of-all-work to a demanding woman who suffered from narcissism and the vapors.

Sir Richard looked at his stepmother, and said to her smoothly, "I am afraid, Marguerite, that I must interfere slightly with your comfort. You see, I had promised your young companion that I would show her Pulteney Bridge and that we would drive out to Sydney Gardens and the hotel tomorrow morning."

Once again he was sparing her sister, thought Marguerite with a guarded gratitude—but why? He was not a considerate man, so it was not because of the kindness of his nature. Of course he had spoken to his stepmother of fear, but his voice had reflected none whatsoever. He was clearly very much in control of the situation. Celia would drive out with him tomorrow, whatever Lady Norwood's plans might have been. She glanced at that lady, and saw that her agreeable mood had vanished like trailing wisps of fog in summer sunshine.

Lady Norwood glared at her stepson. "By whose leave do you interfere with my plans, Richard?" she demanded petulantly. "I want Celia to accompany me tomorrow morning."

Sir Richard met her gaze evenly. "I think, Marguerite,"

he said calmly, but very firmly, "that she will spend it with me."

Celia started to speak—doubtless to say that she would be happy to go with Lady Norwood, her sister thought bitterly—but Sir Richard turned to her.

"Miss Celia, Lady Norwood has Tolliver and your sister to assist her to the Pump Room tomorrow morning, and very likely Dr. Lavenham will also accompany them. Will you not allow me the pleasure of showing you the sights as I promised?"

When appealed to directly, Celia weakened, and she looked at her hostess questioningly. "I could only go, of course, if Lady Norwood felt that she could spare me," she said hesitantly.

Sir Richard directed his steady gaze to his stepmother again. "Well, Marguerite?" he inquired, his voice icy. "Do you feel that you can spare Miss Celia?"

Lady Norwood lifted one shoulder pettishly. "I am sure, Richard, that I could die and you would feel that I needed no one in attendance."

"I assure you, my dear stepmother," he replied blandly, "that if you were dying, I should myself be in attendance. Nothing could keep me from your side."

She stared at him a moment, trying to determine his meaning, and decided to take his comment at face value. "At least you have some family feeling, then," she replied. "I had not thought you would care one way or the other."

"Then you are most inaccurate," Sir Richard returned. "I should care a great deal."

"I suppose that it would be all right, then, child, for you to have a brief outing with Richard. But be certain to be back here by one o'clock," said Lady Norwood, pleased to be able to lay down one requirement at least.

"Of course I shall be," replied Celia, smiling. "And I shall look forward to the drive, Sir Richard."

"You will be in an open carriage, will you not?" demanded Marguerite sharply. It would certainly not do for a lady to go out alone in a closed carriage with a gentleman, as Sir Richard had himself pointed out earlier when he had saved Celia from driving down with Lady Norwood.

"Naturally not, Miss Standish. My tiger brought my curricle down yesterday, and he will be with us."

Relieved of that anxiety—for, although she was doubtful that a tiger and an open carriage made this a perfectly acceptable outing, she felt that if it saved Celia from Lady Norwood's clutches it was the preferable evil—Marguerite was able to give her mind to plans for the next day. It might do her sister a great deal of good to be seen in the company of Sir Richard Norwood, she reflected, her mood growing lighter. Indeed, there might be nothing better. Then, when she did come to the Pump Room, she would be known as someone whom he had singled out for attention. The fact that he did so still bothered Marguerite, of course, but perhaps she could take advantage of it for Celia's sake.

The rest of the evening passed uneventfully and the ladies retired early to bed, weary from their journey. Both of the young ladies looked forward to the coming day, Celia because of the outing she was to have, Marguerite because of the opportunity to inspect the gathering at the Pump Room for marital candidates for Celia.

Eight

True to his promise, Sir Richard and Celia departed in his curricle promptly at ten to take their drive, his small tiger perched behind them. Celia was charmed by the view of Pulteney Bridge from the Grand Parade, white swans floating peacefully beneath its stone arches. Robert Adams' graceful covered bridge, whose domed pavilions at either end balanced the tall Venetian windows in its center, was a fitting introduction to the glory of Great Pulteney Street, one of the most impressive avenues in England.

"I hope that you will enjoy your stay in Bath, Miss Celia," he remarked, enjoying her wide-eyed pleasure.

"If the rest of it is like this morning, Sir Richard, I am certain that I shall," she replied ingenuously.

He smiled. "If I were not acquainted with you, ma'am, I would think that you were casting out lures."

Celia blushed and looked at him earnestly. "But you surely don't believe, Sir Richard—" she began.

He held up his hand. "Not at all, Miss Celia, not for a moment. I know that you were sincere." Noting her stricken expression, he added, "Forgive me. I was merely teasing you, and I should not have done so." His penitence was real, for he had not intended to distress her. He marveled at her simplicity and wondered again how two sisters could be so different in character.

Seeing his sincerity, her color subsided and she was able to smile and to speak without her usual timidity. "No,

Sir Richard. I am the one to be forgiven. Marguerite is always telling me not to be such a goose. I know that I sometimes fly up into the boughs over unimportant things when I should not."

He frowned a little over this as he guided the curricle smartly through the entrance to Sydney Gardens. "May I ask, Miss Celia, what some of the unimportant things are that trouble you? Just why does your sister feel that you are being a goose?"

"It is nothing of consequence, Sir Richard, truly. It is just that—that I am not much accustomed to the company of gentlemen, and I don't know what to say when I am with them."

"But you do very well with me," he remarked.

"That is quite another matter," she assured him confidingly. "You see, you were so kind to me from the first, helping me to take care of Nipper, that I could not be afraid of you. But I know that I must make a good impression when I meet strange gentlemen here, and I'm not certain that I will be able to do so."

His frown deepened. "Why should you have to make a good impression on these unknown gentlemen?" he inquired, certain that he already knew the answer.

"I must marry, you see," she explained. "Marguerite has made my gowns and helped me learn to dance so that I will make a good impression."

"Yes, I do see," Sir Richard replied grimly, determining that he would have a serious talk with Miss Standish before he left Bath. "I'm sure that it would be a good thing for your sister if you were to marry well."

"It would be a good thing for both of us," she returned simply. "We have no home now, and we must have someplace to go when we leave you, so it is my duty to marry."

Sir Richard tightened his grip on the ribbons as he glanced at her troubled expression. He longed to have his talk with Miss Standish as soon as possible, and accordingly he turned the curricle back toward Pulteney Bridge and the Pump Room as soon as they had taken their drive through the gardens. She was not going to sacrifice this child beside him on the marital altar if he could do anything to prevent it. She could very well sacrifice herself instead.

That morning Marguerite had accompanied Lady Norwood to the Pump Room to drink the waters—although Marguerite chose to have tea instead—and she carefully studied the people gathered there. The peak of Bath's season had passed, and Lady Norwood had assured her that the company would be very thin. Knowing that the city was scarcely a magnet for eligible young men even at the height of its season, Marguerite feared that there would be very few marital prospects for Celia. A few minutes, however, were quite enough to make her feel that she need not despair.

They were soon joined by an elegantly attired gentleman that she had noticed immediately upon entering the room. He was a tall man, impeccably groomed, but his movements were lithe and graceful, suggesting the leashed power of a panther. His manner, however, was quite different.

"I was devastated to learn that you were ill, dear lady," he said, bowing over Lady Norwood's hand, "but I am relieved to see that your beauty has not been touched."

Lady Norwood smiled faintly, as though the effort were almost too much for her. "You are merely being kind, Lord Saybrook," she responded. "I am all too aware that I am grown thin and old."

"You!" he exclaimed, in mock horror, his dark eyes amused by this blatant bid for a compliment. "Never! Age shall never dare touch such beauty as yours!" Leaving her to bask in the warmth of his words, he turned to Marguerite and smiled. "And who is this charming young lady?" he inquired.

It was clear from Lady Norwood's expression that she was less than pleased to have his attention diverted from her, and she replied in an offhanded manner, as though the matter were of little consequence. "This is my namesake, Saybrook. Her name is Marguerite Standish, and she and her sister have come to look after me." Then she added, a slight edge to her voice, "Marguerite, you will do well to keep your distance from such a practiced flirt as Lord Saybrook."

Marguerite glanced at her hostess quickly. She knew that Lady Norwood thought of them in just such a manner, scarcely above the status of servants, but she had not expected to hear her put it into words. And she was embarrassed as well by her casual warning against Lord Saybrook.

Lord Saybrook did not miss her glance. "To look after you, Marguerite?" he inquired of Lady Norwood. "Surely you have no need of that. I should imagine that your namesake is here to provide you with her delightful company."

"You see what I mean, Marguerite?" said Lady Norwood dryly. "He is not to be taken seriously." She shrugged and turned away to the young man who had just joined them.

"You must not mind her, you know," said Lord Saybrook in a low voice. "She is accustomed to being the center of attention, as most gazetted beauties are."

Uncertain of what she could reply, Marguerite merely smiled at him, grateful for the quickness of his understanding. He returned the smile, saying, "And I am certain, Miss Standish, that you also must be accustomed to being the center of such attention. I hope that you will be in Bath long enough for us to become better acquainted."

"I see that Lady Norwood was quite right in warning me against you, Lord Saybrook," Marguerite replied lightly. "I shall be very careful."

"I assure you, Miss Standish, that Lady Norwood was most unjust in her description of me," he said in an injured tone. "You would not say that I am a practiced flirt, would you, Miles?" he asked, appealing to the young Adonis in riding clothes who had appeared at his elbow.

The handsome young man seemed to consider the matter for a moment. "No, I don't think that I should say *practiced,* Saybrook," he responded thoughtfully. "Incorrigible, perhaps, would be nearer the mark."

"Do not regard him, Miss Standish," returned Lord Saybrook. "We shall remove ourselves from him immediately before he gives you entirely the wrong impression of me."

And he took Marguerite's elbow, quite as though he intended to steer her away from the rest of the group.

"You will do no such thing, Saybrook," replied his friend firmly. "You will mind your manners and introduce me properly to Miss Standish."

"Very well," sighed Lord Saybrook, removing his hand from her elbow and turning back to the young gentleman. "Miss Standish, I would like to present—actually, of course, I should like *not* to present him, but you see that I have no choice—I am *compelled* to present to you Mr. Miles Randall."

Mr. Randall smiled and bowed. "You must not allow him to trouble you, ma'am," he said, smiling. Marguerite noticed with satisfaction that his eyes smiled, too. "Saybrook is himself accustomed to being the center of attention and having things his own way. He is actually quite harmless, though, no matter how dangerous a fellow he thinks himself."

"As you can see, Miss Standish," interjected Lord Saybrook gravely, "I have no need of enemies so long as I have friends such as Miles. Heaven protect me from my friends!"

Greatly cheered by their banter, Marguerite began to feel that their stay in Bath might very well be more enjoyable than she had feared. In a very brief period of time, they were joined by several other gentlemen, and Marguerite could see that Lady Norwood was accustomed to holding court while in Bath. It would surely be no difficult matter to find a suitable husband for Celia in such a group. She was just wondering about the marital status of the two with whom she had been speaking when Lord Saybrook interrupted her pleasant speculations.

"Miles, do I appear awake to you?" he asked suddenly, raising his quizzing glass to his eye and looking toward the entranceway.

"As much so as ever you do, Saybrook," replied his friend, following his gaze.

"You relieve my mind, dear boy," said Saybrook gravely. "She is real then and not a vision."

Marguerite, too, turned to look at the young lady who was eliciting such a tribute. In the doorway stood Celia on the arm of Sir Richard.

Saybrook lowered his glass and sighed. "I had not noted Norwood's presence or I would have known, of course. *He* would not be a part of my dreams."

Sir Richard and Celia made their way across the room to join Lady Norwood, Sir Richard pointedly ignoring the outer fringes of the circle where Marguerite stood with Saybrook and his friends.

"Do you know the vision, Miss Standish?" inquired Saybrook of Marguerite, seeing Celia smile and wave in their direction.

Marguerite smiled. "She is my sister," she replied, thinking that this was all so much easier than she had thought it would be. Finding a suitable husband for Celia seemed now a very real possibility.

Lord Saybrook blinked. "Forgive me, Miss Standish," he said, sweeping a low bow, "that I so far forgot myself as to give my attention to another young lady when you are present."

"It was not well done of you, Saybrook," agreed Miles

gravely. "I was wondering when you would remember your manners."

"I regret to say that for once, Miles, you are absolutely correct. My behavior was unforgivable."

Marguerite laughed. It was impossible to take him seriously. "I have long been accustomed to watching others admire Celia, Lord Saybrook," she assured him. "It does not distress me. Indeed, I do not see how one could do other than admire her."

"Celia," murmured Miles to no one in particular, still staring at the vision. "How very fitting a name, for she is celestial." Oblivious now to the others, and no more mindful of his manners than his friend had been, he stood staring in Celia's direction.

Saybrook smiled at Marguerite. "Now you must overlook *his* behavior, Miss Standish. He is young, you see, and callow." He paused a moment, his dark eyes thoughtful as he looked down at her. "Forgive me for saying so, ma'am, but it is a rare thing for a young lady to be so lacking in jealousy when another young lady—even her own sister—is admired."

"I could not be jealous of Celia, Lord Saybrook," she replied. "You don't know her. She doesn't even believe that she *is* beautiful. It isn't something she thinks about."

Lord Saybrook smiled, his expression revealing his disbelief. "Ah, now, Miss Standish, you have pressed the boundaries of belief too far. For a young lady not to know of her own beauty and her power over others is unheard of. Beauties such as she learn that power in the cradle."

"Not Celia," replied Marguerite. "You will see."

He bowed, clearly still not believing her. "As you say, Miss Standish. I shall look forward to making the acquaintance of this paragon."

Accordingly, Marguerite introduced both Saybrook and Miles to her sister, and a brief conversation ensued. Celia spoke but seldom and Sir Richard removed all of their party in fairly short order.

After their return to the Royal Crescent, Marguerite was startled by an abrupt invitation from Sir Richard to join him for a brief drive to Beechen Cliff, which overlooked the city.

"I believe that you will appreciate the view, ma'am," he informed her briskly, as the curricle crossed the Old Bath Bridge and headed into the country.

"I'm sure that I shall, Sir Richard," she replied cautiously. "It is very kind of you to invite me." Even though he had shown himself capable of being a charming host, she still could not trust his pleasant demeanor.

"Your sister assured me that you would enjoy it above all things," he said. "She seems to be very aware of your thinking upon most subjects."

Marguerite laughed. "We have lived too long together, you see," she replied. "We know each other's every thought."

He did not reply, but gave her a most curious glance. The reason for it became quite evident to her within a very brief period of time. She noticed that his tiger had not joined them on their drive, and she remarked upon that to Sir Richard.

"You had indicated to me earlier, Miss Standish, that you did not care to discuss private matters in front of servants," he replied grimly.

She flushed, remembering the circumstances of that remark. "I must take it then, that you are about to be unpleasant again, Sir Richard."

"I am certain that you will think so, Miss Standish. I wish to speak to you about your sister."

"Indeed?" she said coolly, her eyebrows raised. "And what might you have to say to me about such a private matter, Sir Richard?"

"I wonder if you realize how uneasy she is about becoming marriage bait in your little game, Miss Standish," he remarked, flicking his whip neatly over his leader's ear as they took a deep curve.

"What do you mean by that, Sir Richard?" she demanded. "I cannot believe that Celia would ever use such an expression as 'marriage bait'! That must be your own doing."

He bowed in her direction. "I must indeed take credit," he returned. "As you say, your sister would never have used such an expression. And she thinks so highly of you that she will do anything you ask of her, including learning to dance and dress in a manner that will please the gentlemen."

Marguerite flushed even more deeply. "You make this sound a great deal more reprehensible than it is, Sir Richard," she replied. "You know quite well that young ladies of your set do precisely that and no one thinks the less of them."

"Your sister is of a finer quality than many of them," he returned, ignoring the justice of her remark. "She feels very uncomfortable about trying to do such things—she isn't suited to playing the game, Miss Standish. You must surely see that."

Since Marguerite had begun to have much the same uncomfortable thoughts herself, hearing them come from Sir Richard did not endear him to her. "I would never force her to marry where she does not love, sir," she returned defensively. "Celia knows that."

"I think that you underestimate her love for you, Miss Standish. She perceives marriage to be her duty so that she will be able to take care of both of you. She will do it."

Mortified by the truth of his statement, Marguerite sat silently for the next two miles.

Finally, the silence was broken by Sir Richard. His voice sounded as though he were having to labor to keep his tone restrained and calm. "And I wonder, Miss Standish, if you realize to whom you were introducing your young sister this morning at the Pump Room."

"Yes, of course," she replied, puzzled by his question. "Lord Saybrook and Mr. Miles Randall. I had myself just met them."

"And, knowing nothing of them, you deliberately made them known to your young sister?"

"What are you saying, Sir Richard?" she demanded. "What is it that I should know about them?"

"Of Miles Randall, nothing at all. But of Saybrook!" He pulled the curricle up sharply, ignoring the magnificent view of Bath below them and glaring down at Marguerite. "Saybrook is the most dangerous of men for a young girl like Celia."

Marguerite took angry note of the fact that he called her sister by her first name, but she did not refer to it. "Dangerous?" she said in disbelief. "How is he dangerous? He seemed very charming—he has, in fact, manners far more agreeable than your own, Sir Richard!"

"Of course he does, Miss Standish!" he snapped. "I am no womanizer! And he uses those charming manners to advantage. He is not to be trusted with any young woman, particularly one so innocent of the world as your sister! You might as well send a lamb in to play with a tiger!"

Suddenly recalling the manner in which Saybrook moved, and the mental comparison she had made when she first saw him, Marguerite was at first shaken, but a moment or two of thought allowed her to rally.

"And yet Lady Norwood is a good friend of a man with such a reprehensible reputation?" she demanded. "You do not like your stepmother, Sir Richard, but this is pressing matters a little too far. Surely she would not allow such a man into her intimate circle of friends."

Sir Richard laughed. "I see that you still do not know my stepmother well, Miss Standish. So long as he pays court to her, any man is welcome in her 'intimate circle.'

You would do well to remember that. And you would do well to keep your sister away from that circle."

"I note, Sir Richard, that you do not say that I would do well to keep myself away," she observed dryly. "Is there a particular reason for that?"

He gave her a short bow. "But of course, Miss Standish. I have seen from the first that you are formed of a different metal from your sister. I have no doubt that you will handle yourself very well in any situation. You are, after all, my stepmother's namesake. Why should I expect your behavior to be any different from hers?"

And so saying he transferred the ribbons to his left hand, reached down and, with his right arm, caught her to him and kissed her firmly. "And if you persist in driving out alone with a man, Miss Standish, you might as well know the kind of behavior you may expect. Consider this a lesson."

With that he directed the curricle onto the road and back toward town, not deigning to glance down at his furious passenger again. Marguerite was seething at the insults he had heaped upon her, but she could think of nothing to say that would not make her sound petulant and spoiled or self-righteously indignant. He was right, of course, about going out alone with a gentleman. She had known that when she had seen that the tiger was not present—not that having the tiger along really made a difference. She should not have gone—and she should not have allowed Celia to go either. At least she knew that he had not behaved in such a manner with Celia.

Try as she would, she could think of nothing to say that would put him properly in his place. Not for an instant did she believe his warnings against Lord Saybrook. A man with manners such as his was scarcely likely to make such an innocent as Celia his victim. Admire her, yes. Flirt with her, yes. But to do more than that was inconceivable to Marguerite. She would never have expected the sort of Turkish treatment she had just received at the hands of Sir Richard from Lord Saybrook.

It disturbed her, though, that she was now wondering whether or not she had done the proper thing for Celia in bringing her here. Perhaps Sir Richard was right in his belief that she should not have been placed in such a situation.

The most disturbing thing about the drive with Sir Richard, however, was the fact that she had not found his kiss distasteful. His manner, yes—but his nearness, not at all. It was just as well, she reflected, that he was about to leave Bath. He might speak of the dangers of Lord Saybrook—but he was by far the more dangerous man.

Nine

It was with relief that she learned the next morning that Sir Richard had departed. He had not troubled himself to take leave of her, of course, but he had said his farewells to Celia.

"He left me his direction at Greenwood Park, Marguerite," she said wonderingly. "And he told me how to go about sending him a message there should I have need of him. That was very kind of him, was it not?"

Marguerite did not reply immediately, thinking angrily that he had undoubtedly meant she was to notify him if she were being forced into a marriage against her will, and Celia added, "I cannot think why I might have need of him, though. Do you think that he meant I might call upon him if I were about to transport Nipper again?"

"No doubt," replied her sister abruptly. "I am certain that you could ask anything of Sir Richard, no matter how trivial, and he would come flying to take care of the matter for you."

Celia stared at Marguerite and her eyes filled. "Have I said something that I ought not, Marguerite?" she asked, her voice trembling. "You sound so angry."

Marguerite patted her hand contritely. "Pay no attention to me, Celia. Of course you have done nothing amiss. How could you?"

Comforted, Celia returned to her toast and tea, for they were once again breakfasting alone. Lady Norwood would not put in an appearance until it was time to depart for the Pump Room. Marguerite, feeling insensibly cheered because the specter of Sir Richard had been removed and she no longer had to fear encountering him at every turn, began to look forward to the day. They would undoubtedly see some of those they had met in the Pump Room the day before, and she enjoyed just the thought of hearing pleasant conversation and being able to watch so many people gathered together in one place. It was a far cry from their limited activities at Northaven.

"I had not realized how much I truly disliked living in Northaven," she remarked aloud. "Aren't you enjoying the variety of people and scenes here in Bath?" she asked her sister.

Celia was silent for a moment. "I know that I should be," she returned slowly, "but I cannot help feeling that this is not—not a very comfortable way to live, Marguerite. I should not like to live so all the time."

Dismayed, Marguerite turned the conversation immediately to Nipper and to the possibility of a walk in the Crescent Fields later that afternoon, things that would cheer Celia and divert her thoughts in a more positive direction. It could be, she thought unhappily, that Sir Richard was right and that she should not have uprooted Celia. She put that thought firmly from her mind, however, as she thought of Vincent Beezley. It was simply that everything here was so new to them. How could she expect Celia to adjust so quickly? Time was all that was required.

She was less certain of that at the Pump Room later that morning, for the gentlemen were clustering about them, and Celia scarcely spoke three words during the whole of the time. That she was admired was obvious to all of them, including Lady Norwood, who did not seem to be particularly pleased with the attention bestowed upon her guest.

Lord Saybrook and a newcomer to the group, a Mr. Tavistock, had been arguing about whether or not Celia's eyes were the cerulean blue of the sky in May or in mid-summer. This had been the subject of a lively debate for some few minutes, with Lady Norwood growing more restive with the passing of each moment.

"Tell me, Miles," said Saybrook, appealing to his friend for support, "would you not say that the blue of Miss Standish's eyes makes you think of the peaceful, deep blue of a midsummer sky—the sort of blueness that you could drown in?"

"Not a bit of it," interrupted Tavistock before Miles could speak. "The blue of a May sky is full of promise—it is tender and alluring."

"I think," replied Miles firmly, "that Miss Standish's eyes have the look of someone longing for a glass of lemonade and a change of subject. May I, ma'am?" he said, bowing and offering her his arm.

To Marguerite's surprise, Celia smiled gratefully and took his arm, allowing him to lead her away from the group and toward the refreshments. Undoubtedly she was ready to welcome any respite from the attention she had been receiving.

Saybrook and Tavistock watched them go, openmouthed. "Why, the impudence of the puppy!" exclaimed Saybrook, holding up his quizzing glass to stare after them. "I shall be obliged to call him out! I had not yet made my best points, and now Miss Standish shall not hear them."

"That is just as well, Saybrook," replied Lady Norwood petulantly. "We had heard quite enough of your maudlin tributes to her eyes. Surely you could find something more worthwhile to talk about."

Saybrook bowed to her, his eyes sparkling mischievously. "But, of course, dear Marguerite. I was just about to mention that *your* eyes are summer eyes as well. I am aware, however, that you are far too knowing to accept such overblown compliments. You have received the homage of too many men skilled in the art of dalliance to appreciate my poor efforts."

"You underrate yourself, Saybrook," she replied lazily, more pleasantly disposed as soon as she was once again the focus of attention. "I am prepared to be amused by your attempts."

She glanced at Marguerite and waved vaguely in the direction taken by Celia and Miles. "Why don't you look after your sister, Marguerite?" she inquired.

Understanding that Lady Norwood wished to be left entirely alone with her admirers—and thus the center of their attention—Marguerite overlooked the dismissive tone she had used, and went in search of Celia.

To her surprise, she found her sister talking shyly with Miles Randall, telling him of their life in Northaven and—of all things—of their mother's garden and of taking care of the ducks and geese early on spring mornings. Judging by the gentleman's rapt expression, he had heard no more fascinating tale in many months. She wondered for a moment about this young man's reputation. Sir Richard had expended most of his venom on Lord Saybrook and had never moved on to vilifying Miles Randall. He had an open, pleasant countenance, and aside from the fact that he was extremely handsome and a friend of Saybrook's, she knew of nothing against him. That, coupled with the fact that he had rescued Celia and actually succeeded in drawing her into conversation, disposed her kindly toward him.

"Listening to tales about home, I see," she remarked cheerfully as she joined them.

"Yes, it sounds charming, Miss Standish," said Miles enthusiastically. "I had never realized that tending ducks and geese could be so enjoyable."

"Not everyone feels that it is, Mr. Randall," replied Marguerite. "I fear that I am one that does not enjoy it. Celia, as you can see, feels far otherwise. She had named every bird there and fully half of them recognized their names when she called and would come waddling over to her whenever she appeared."

"I can understand that," said Miles, smiling. "I feel that I would respond in much the same way."

"Surely not, Miles," remonstrated a shocked voice from behind Marguerite. "Not by waddling over to her, surely. You are usually far more graceful than that. I must defend you from yourself."

Miles blushed. "You know what I meant, Saybrook," he responded lightly. "And I hope that Miss Standish—both the Miss Standishes," he amended, bowing to Marguerite, "understood my meaning more clearly than you apparently did."

Celia smiled gently and Marguerite laughed. "Of course we did, Mr. Randall. I see, however, that Lord Saybrook must forever be entertaining himself at the expense of others."

Lord Saybrook held up his hands in protest. "Indeed I do not, Miss Standish! I would never, for instance, dream of entertaining myself at *your* expense. Miles, however, has always made himself so very available for my amusement that it has seemed churlish not to take advantage of his invitation."

Marguerite did not hear Miles' rejoinder clearly, for Tolliver suddenly materialized at her elbow and said in a low, sharp voice, "My lady wishes for you and your sister to join her in the carriage immediately and not to be keeping her waiting when she is feeling so ill."

Seeing Marguerite's startled glance, Tolliver nodded in bleak satisfaction. "Had a very bad spell just a moment ago, miss—and all because of the thoughtlessness of you and your sister. You'd best come along right now if you don't wish to be walking home." And she departed as abruptly as she had appeared.

Marguerite had no doubt as to the reason for Lady Norwood's sudden sinking spell. When she had found herself deserted by her admirers, even Saybrook departing to pay court to Celia, she had certainly been infuriated. Marguerite sighed. This would not be a pleasant journey home.

Making their excuses to the others, they hurried to the carriage and sat quietly in the corner while Tolliver ministered to her mistress, who was reclining on one of the seats.

"Just see what your selfishness has brought on," said Tolliver angrily. "She has no more strength than a kitten and what must the two of you do but gad about the Pump Room without a single thought for her!"

Marguerite was quite unmoved, but Celia's eyes filled with tears. "I am so sorry, Lady Norwood," she said. "Do let me bathe your temples."

Lady Norwood motioned her away with her hand. "Tolliver can take care of me very well, thank you. *She* is devoted to my interests." Noting with satisfaction that Celia had felt the power of this dart, she continued, "I would have thought that those I brought into my home to care for out of the goodness of my heart would have shown as much consideration, but I see that it was not to be."

This barb cut Celia to the quick, but Marguerite interceded before she could speak. "I am sure that some rest and quiet are what you need, Lady Norwood," she said quietly, "so as soon as we are back at the Crescent, Celia and I will go out in order that you may have some time to yourself."

Lady Norwood certainly had no desire for her two charges to stroll out and enjoy themselves while she was confined to her home, but she could not think of any immediate retort and so lapsed into sullen silence for the short duration of their journey.

Once within the confines of her house, however, Lady Norwood had a pleasant surprise that revived her and made her, at least for the moment, almost cheerful. In the drawing room waited a young man whose golden beauty lighted the room. Marguerite and Celia, being well-bred young ladies, did not stare, but it was difficult not to do so.

His head belongs on a Grecian coin, thought Marguerite, admiring the perfection of his features. He was immaculately dressed, from his faultless boots to his crisply starched, intricately arranged neckcloth.

"Philippe!" exclaimed Lady Norwood, holding out her arms to him. "My dearest boy, how very glad I am to see you!"

He gave her the briefest of embraces, apparently fearful of disarranging the perfection of his sartorial splendor, thought Marguerite, not quite as impressed with him as she had been at first. Then he slipped out of her arms and gazed at the two sisters still standing in the doorway.

"So these are the young ladies you have told me about, Mama," he said. "How delightful it is to have you here." Approaching them, he extended his hand gracefully and bowed to each of them, kissing their hands lightly in the French fashion. "I am Philippe Norwood, ladies—or, as I am sure you know, the Marquis de Valencia, although I do not claim that title publicly."

"I have told Philippe it is not wise to do so just yet," observed his mother fondly. "England is filled with Frenchmen claiming nonexistent titles. When the war is over with, we will be able to straighten out our affairs in France. Then Philippe will claim what is rightfully his."

"That seems a wise approach," murmured Marguerite, rather surprised that her hostess would be so practical. "Although it must be difficult to wait, Mr. Norwood."

"Oh, it is indeed!" he exclaimed, giving her a look of appreciation. "I think that most people do not realize what a sacrifice I am making, Miss Standish—but please call me Philippe. After all, Mama tells me that we are practically brother and sister."

"Very well—Philippe," returned Marguerite, a little hesitantly. She wondered uncomfortably if his mother was indeed aware that there was a very close relationship between them. In any case, he seemed almost too enthusiastic to suit her tastes. "Will you be long in Bath?"

"I shall be here as long as you ladies are," he replied gaily. "I am here to be at your disposal, ready to run errands, to conduct you on outings, to leave myself at your beck and call."

Marguerite viewed this as very hopeful news, thinking that there might well be more of a social life than she had feared. Thus far their outings had been limited to the Pump Room and there had been no mention of any evening activities. Perhaps Philippe would make a difference in their plans.

"I am afraid, Philippe," said his mother in a weakened voice, "that I have had a relapse and have not been feeling at all the thing. I fear that I will not be able to go out very much for some time."

"Nonsense, Mama!" he responded stoutly. "I daresay that some activity is precisely what you are needing. I will have you on your feet in no time at all."

His mother appeared to react positively to his words, and Marguerite grew more hopeful still. She was quite sure that Lady Norwood's relapse was no more than a fit of jealousy brought about by the attention that Celia had been receiving—attention that she felt properly belonged to her. Perhaps now, with Philippe's presence, things could go on a little more smoothly. There would be more pleasant matters to occupy her attention.

"Mama tells me that she and your mother were very dear friends, and that we are even very distantly related," said Philippe, turning back to Marguerite.

"Yes, that is true," she nodded, smiling, thinking to herself that she hoped the relationship truly was a distant one. The more she saw of Lady Norwood, the less closely related to her she wished to be.

He studied her for a moment, then Celia, then nodded

judiciously. "I think that I can see it," he said seriously. "We have the same delicate cast of the features, the same graceful bone structure." Marguerite, who had made the same study, had reached quite a different conclusion, but she did not say anything.

"Tell me, Marguerite dear," interrupted his mother. "I had nearly forgotten this matter. Have you the locket that you wrote to me about? The one with the miniatures of my parents? I know that Philippe would be most anxious to see it."

"A locket?" he exclaimed. "Indeed I would like to see it, Marguerite."

Celia looked at her in bewilderment, and Marguerite realized suddenly that she had never told her about the locket, having wished to avoid the matter of Mama's illegitimate birth.

"Let me go up to my chamber and get it," she said smoothly. "I think that we need to freshen up a bit at any rate. Will you come with me, Celia?" she inquired, smiling at her sister.

Celia nodded and followed her silently up the steps to her bedchamber. Closing the door firmly behind her, Marguerite whispered earnestly, "I found the locket in Mama's trunk and wrote to Lady Norwood about it. I believe that the locket is the reason we were invited here."

"But, Marguerite, why didn't you show it to me?" asked Celia, her expression hurt.

"It was because of the miniature of Lady Norwood's mother, dear. She looked—well, she looked almost exactly like Mama and like you."

Celia stared at her, puzzled. "Like Mama and me?" she inquired slowly. "Why would that be? Lady Norwood does not look particularly like us."

"I don't want to upset you, my dear, but it occurred to me that Mama might have been illegitimate—and more nearly related to the Marquise than we realized. Such things happen, you know, and Mama never seemed to wish to speak of her childhood—perhaps she didn't want Papa to know."

Celia grew pale at the thought. "Indeed she would not have wished him to know," she breathed. "How terrible for Mama to have had to keep such a secret!"

"Well, I didn't wish to tell you, Celia, because I was afraid that it would upset you as well."

Celia shook her head. "I am quite all right. I would like to see the miniatures though."

It was Marguerite's turn to shake her head. "I'm afraid that is impossible now, Celia. I appear to have lost the locket."

"Lost it!" exclaimed Celia. "How could you have lost it, Marguerite?"

"I don't know," she answered honestly. "I have no idea how it could have happened, but I realized when we first arrived that I had mislaid it. It is possible, I suppose, that I lost it the day I was packing. It could still be back at the rectory."

"Then we must write to Mr. Clive!" exclaimed Celia.

"Just so," agreed her sister. "And I shall do so immediately. I am going to look through my luggage one last time before going down to confess to Lady Norwood. Why don't you go across to your room to freshen up?"

Celia departed, and Marguerite turned back to her luggage. Swiftly she opened her sewing basket and made a tiny slit in its lining, taking the locket from her reticule where she had carefully kept it with her day and night, and sliding it into the stuffing that padded the basket's lining. Threading a tiny needle, she stitched up the slit, making her stitches so minute that no one would have noticed it, while the stuffing disguised the presence of the locket.

She had decided while listening to Lady Norwood that afternoon that she did not wish to allow this lady to have the locket. To be sure, it was rightfully hers—still, it did not feel quite right to turn it over to her. Besides, this was still her only likeness of Mama and Celia. She would tell Lady Norwood that she had lost it, and if she changed her mind about that lady, she could always "find" the locket in her luggage. She had decided to keep it a secret from Celia, too, because her sister was too transparent to keep a secret of any sort. Perhaps when their visit was over and they were safely away from Lady Norwood, she would take it out and show Celia.

Telling their hostess about its loss was quite as distasteful as she had feared it would be.

"Lost! How could you have been so careless?" Lady Norwood exclaimed. "When did you see it last?"

"When I was packing at the rectory," responded Marguerite contritely. "I will write to Mr. Clive, the present rector, immediately, and ask him to search for it."

Lady Norwood lay back among the cushions on her sofa and studied Marguerite. "You do not seem to me to be a careless person, Marguerite," she said slowly. "Are you quite certain that you have searched everywhere possible among your things?"

Marguerite nodded. "It simply is not where I thought I had packed it. I cannot tell you how sorry I am, Lady Norwood." That much at least is true, she thought.

"Have you thought back to the time you last saw it," interceded Philippe, "and tried to trace your steps from that point?"

Marguerite nodded again, closing her eyes as though picturing her movements. "It simply does not appear in my recollection of the events afterwards," she said. "I am sorry, for I know that you would have loved to see the miniatures."

He nodded eagerly. "I have so few things to remind me of my heritage, you see, and so this would have been an important link for me." He, too, appeared to study her face. "If you think of anything, anything at all that might be helpful in finding it, you will tell us, won't you, Marguerite? I would be most happy to send a messenger to check in any place you might have left it."

Marguerite nodded, hating herself for being so duplicitous, yet she could not bring herself to simply give them the locket.

"Where were you planning to carry it on your journey?" asked Lady Norwood suddenly, and Marguerite looked up, startled.

"Why—I was going to carry it in my reticule," she responded. "I felt that since I had that with me at all times, it would be safest there."

"And you have searched the contents of your reticule carefully?" she demanded.

Again Marguerite nodded. "It is not there," she replied firmly.

"There could have been a small tear in the lining, you know," persisted Lady Norwood. "Did you check to see if it could be in the lining?"

At the mention of the lining, Marguerite felt herself flush faintly and hoped that no one else had noticed. "There is no tear, Lady Norwood," she replied firmly. "The locket is not in the lining, nor could it have simply dropped from the reticule."

Dissatisfied, but unable to think of any other questions, Lady Norwood was obliged to let the matter drop. Relieved to realize that the inquisition was over, Marguerite noticed for the first time that Tolliver was in the room, a dark shadow hovering in the background—and smiling at her discomfiture.

The rest of the day passed pleasantly enough, for Marguerite visited with Philippe for a while, listening to his ambitious stories of what he would do once the war with France was over with, and then he escorted them for a

stroll across the broad pavement in front of the Royal
Crescent and then down across the green of the Crescent
Fields. It was, naturally, a pleasure for Celia, and Marguerite enjoyed watching her sister's delight. It was not
precisely a surprise when they encountered Miles Randall
also strolling across the Fields—at least it was not a surprise to Marguerite. She rather suspected that he had been
watching for Celia to emerge from the house so that he
could casually encounter her once more.

Marguerite was wondering about Mr. Randall and wishing that she knew more about him as she went upstairs
to change for dinner. She noticed uneasily that a few of
the articles on her dressing table were slightly rearranged,
but she shrugged that off, knowing that the maid could
be responsible for the slight shifting. Still, she opened her
sewing basket and checked carefully. The locket was still
there, but the contents of the basket were tumbled together
rather than in their normal order. Certainly the maid would
have had no reason to open the basket, she thought slowly,
returning the articles to their proper places.

Suddenly she remembered the anonymous note she had
received and opened her lap desk. She had secreted it
inside a small leather volume of poetry, and placed that
securely inside the lap desk and fastened the hasp.

The book was still there, but the note was gone.

As she replaced the book and secured the hasp, Marguerite noticed with a detached interest that her hand was trembling. Almost she could understand their searching for the
locket. Perhaps they suspected that she was lying—perhaps
suspected that she was a thief. But who would take the
anonymous note except its author? And what would they
say if they now discovered the locket? Would she be accused of theft? Or, at the very least, rank ingratitude?

Marguerite dressed for dinner very slowly that evening,
trying to think matters through logically. The culprit could,
of course, be Lady Norwood, although it seemed unlikely

that she would lower herself to searching the room of a guest. Or it could be Tolliver, sent on the errand by her mistress or perhaps undertaking it on her own because of her jealousy of the newcomers. It could even be Philippe, for although he had spent most of the afternoon with them, it would have been no problem for him to slip upstairs and search her room while they were still engaged in conversation with Lady Norwood. The only person she could now eliminate from suspicion was Sir Richard, and Marguerite could find small comfort there. In fact, she would have preferred to suspect him. Such an action would fit with her picture of him.

Checking her sewing basket one more time, she left it in its prominent place on a table beside her bed, trusting that it would now be ignored, and left the room to join Celia before going down to dinner. All that she could do now was to pretend that she had truly lost the locket.

Ten

The next few days passed without incident, and Marguerite had the pleasure of seeing Celia become slightly more comfortable with their visits to the Pump Room. Miles Randall was still the only gentleman with whom she would actually converse, but the others, led by Lord Saybrook, had the enjoyment of studying her lovely countenance while they were attempting to display their wit and tell their anecdotes for her enjoyment.

Marguerite had been pleased to learn from Mrs. Tremble, an elderly, gossipy lady she had met at the Pump Room, that Miles Randall was the only son of a landed gentleman living just to the east of Bath, and that he was considered a most eligible bachelor. "He broke several hearts during the season just past," confided Mrs. Tremble, "and I daresay he didn't even realize it. He is not a hardened flirt like Saybrook."

Feeling that she could encourage Mr. Randall with a clear conscience, Marguerite had allowed him to walk with them to Milsom Street when she had an errand to run, and even to go with them the two miles to the village of Weston and back. When he had discovered that they wished for more exercise than they had been able to take within the confines of the city, it had been Mr. Randall who had suggested this particular walk and had volunteered to escort them. Lady Norwood had not demurred and Philippe was not in the habit of exerting himself in such a manner, so the three of them had spent a cheerful afternoon enjoying the brightness of the weather and the ease of one another's company.

Marguerite could only marvel at the natural way in which Celia was able to chat with him. To be sure, he encouraged her to talk of home, and of her animals, and he had been paid the supreme compliment of being invited to call at the Crescent and make the acquaintance of Nipper. Marguerite had a mental picture of how pleased Lady Norwood would be, both to see Mr. Randall calling upon Celia instead of upon her, and to see Nipper's cage arriving in the drawing room so that the proper introductions could be made.

The scene, when it occurred the next morning, was much as she had pictured it. Lady Norwood looked dismayed when Nipper was brought into the room, but when the conversation centered around the clever, confiding way he hopped upon Mr. Randall's finger and nibbled a biscuit being held for his refreshment, she began to look distinctly like a thundercloud. When Lord Saybrook joined them a few moments later, upbraiding Miles for stealing a march on the rest of them, the storm broke.

"I will not have that bird in my drawing room, free to scatter feathers and seed and—and other disgusting matter about the room!" she said sharply. "Return it to its cage and take it to your room, Celia!"

Celia, surprised by the anger of her tone, hastened to obey her, but Nipper had not liked the sound of Lady Norwood's voice either. Agitated, he flew to the chandelier and perched there, scolding Lady Norwood shrilly.

Lord Saybrook collapsed on a graceful Grecian sofa and succumbed to laughter. "I must say, Marguerite, you need to use a sweeter tone if you expect to lure anyone to your side—man or beast. *I* thought you sounded a little sour just now, and it appears that the bird did not care for your tone of voice either."

"Saybrook, this is no time for your attempts at wit!" exclaimed Lady Norwood angrily. "I will thank you to leave my drawing room immediately!"

Lord Saybrook settled back comfortably on the sofa. "Marguerite, I have not been this entertained for some time. Don't think for a moment that I will leave until I see what happens here."

Knowing that she could not risk his wrath by calling in a footman to eject him bodily, Lady Norwood had to satisfy her own anger by turning on the others about her whom she could control.

"Well, don't just stand there like a stick, Philippe!" she cried. "Get that bird down off of the chandelier."

He looked at her in bewilderment. "How would you suggest that I do that, Mother?" he inquired. "It is quite beyond my reach."

In the corner Mr. Tavistock was carefully removing his handsome Hessian boots. "Come here, Saybrook," he commanded, climbing onto one of the sofas. "I shall stand on your shoulders and capture the little beast."

Saybrook's shoulders shook with laughter. "I think not, Tavistock. Ruin a perfectly good jacket and neckcloth by letting you scrabble about all over me? Besides, I have been laughing so hard that I would doubtless drop you on your head and then Lady Norwood would be obliged to send for a surgeon. Worse still, you might get blood on the carpet."

Tavistock, deflated, seated himself to draw his boots back on. In the meantime, Nipper had taken offense to the actions of one of the footmen, who, responding to Lady Norwood's frantic ringing and entering into the spirit of the occasion, was energetically flipping a long linen cloth in the direction of the chandelier. The only thing accomplished by this was that the chandelier was rocking precariously and Lord Saybrook appeared dangerously near a fit of apoplexy.

Nipper, taking umbrage at the Turkish treatment he was receiving, flew to the top of a pier glass, balanced there a moment, and then alighted on the relative security of Miles Randall's shoulder. Gratefully, Celia held out her finger and Nipper stepped daintily onto it, looking longingly toward the safety of his cage.

It was at this inauspicious moment that a voice from the door said gravely, "I see that I have arrived at a time of great activity."

Startled, the others in the room looked up to see Sir Richard surveying them from the entryway.

"Richard!" exclaimed Lady Norwood. "I thought that you were at Greenwood Park!"

"I believe that she meant *safely* at Greenwood Park, Norwood," interjected Lord Saybrook helpfully.

Sir Richard afforded him no more than a cursory glance before turning to Celia. "May I be of assistance, Celia?" he inquired, reaching out to take the cage. "Perhaps I could take Nipper back to your chamber for you before there is another scene."

To the chagrin of the other gentlemen, he led Celia from the drawing room, Nipper in tow. Marguerite rose unobtrusively and followed them.

"I believe that we have been bested," remarked Lord Saybrook casually. "I had no idea that Norwood had grown so protective, Marguerite, nor that Miss Standish had such a claim on his affections."

"Nonsense!" snapped Lady Norwood. "He is just being difficult, as he always is. He doesn't care a fig for anyone save himself."

Lord Saybrook looked thoughtful. "And I would have agreed with you until just a moment ago. Now, however, I somehow doubt that is true, Marguerite. I believe that you had best take a closer look at the matter."

Leaving their hostess to gather her startled thoughts, Lord Saybrook and the others made their departure. When

Sir Richard re-entered the drawing room a few moments later, he announced briskly, "I have a business matter to attend to, Marguerite, but you need not worry that I will be staying here with you. I have already taken rooms at the White Hart."

"Well, thank heavens for that," remarked Philippe frankly. "It is a good deal too cramped to have you and your retinue move in, Richard."

Sir Richard studied his brother silently for a moment. "You look well, Philippe," he remarked.

"And why should I not, my dear brother?" inquired Philippe archly. "I can think of no possible reason that I should look other than well."

"I am glad to hear it," replied Sir Richard. "You relieve my mind."

"You take too much upon yourself, Richard!" exclaimed Lady Norwood sharply. "You behave as though Philippe is forever getting himself in the briars! You have not been called upon to help him in some time!"

He bowed. "It has indeed been at least four months since I have been dunned by one of Philippe's creditors," he agreed amiably. "I hold the fond hope that we may run another four months."

Here he eyed his half brother sharply and Philippe flushed. "Just as I thought," Norwood remarked grimly. "How much will it be this time?"

"I would prefer to speak of this privately," replied Philippe, attempting to muster some dignity.

"You could be right," nodded Sir Richard. "No doubt it would be unsettling to your mother to know the weightiness of your obligations."

The two gentlemen stepped into the library to complete their conversation, leaving Lady Norwood to fret in the drawing room. Impatiently, she rang for Tolliver to massage her temples in an attempt to pass the time. When she heard her son issue from the room, she rushed to the doorway and beckoned him to come in, shutting the door behind him.

"Did he treat you very terribly?" she asked sympathetically, attempting to brush back one of his handsome golden curls from his forehead.

Philippe pulled away impatiently. "No more so than he usually does," he said petulantly. "He has no understanding of what it is to have to live on such a very small allowance. He could not do it himself."

"Of course he could not," agreed his mother. "We both know what Richard is and what he is willing to do for money."

They looked at each other for a moment, then Philippe nodded. "We do, of course. It is a pity that what we are the ones that look grasping. There was no reason for him to inherit virtually everything."

They both sat for a moment in silence, considering the unfairness of their position.

"He is going to join us at the theater tonight," he added bitterly. "That will enliven our party immeasurably. There is nothing like Richard's austere presence to cast a damper over things."

The theater party was all that Philippe expected it to be. Celia and Marguerite were pleased beyond measure by their first visit to the Theatre Royal, and Philippe had been prepared to bask in their gratitude. Now, however, he felt at a distinct disadvantage with Richard present. He felt younger, less sure of himself. And it was no help when they were joined by a bevy of admirers during the interval. Lady Norwood was in a dark mood because the gentlemen were clearly there to attend Celia and Marguerite, and Philippe was all but pressed from his own box by the interlopers.

Sir Richard had withdrawn to the passageway and stood

watching the group cynically. He could see that Marguerite was in her element, bantering with Saybrook and Tavistock, while Celia sat quietly in her corner, not responding to their sallies with anything save a smile until Miles Randall made his way close enough to exchange a word with her.

"What a very lovely child, Norwood," said Saybrook on his way out of the box. "And her sister is charming, too," he added, nodding in Marguerite's direction. "I noticed, however, that you seem to fancy the younger one. I compliment you, Norwood. You have impeccable taste."

"You forget yourself, sir," said Norwood stiffly. "You are speaking of a lady."

"Stiff as a stick, aren't you?" observed Saybrook sympathetically. "But then you always were. It must make courting the young lady very difficult for you." And he ambled casually down the passageway to chat with Randall and Tavistock.

Marguerite had a delightful evening at the theater. She had feared that Sir Richard would change the atmosphere and spoil her first opportunity truly to enjoy herself, but he had not. On the contrary, he had said almost nothing during the course of the evening.

To her surprise and that of all of the inhabitants of the house on Royal Crescent, Sir Richard accompanied them home and came in with them. Lady Norwood announced that she was retiring immediately and Sir Richard merely nodded.

"May I have a word with you, Miss Standish?" he said to Marguerite.

Startled by his request, she merely nodded.

"With your permission, I will borrow the use of your library for a few minutes," said Sir Richard, turning to his stepmother. She nodded, and made her way up the stairs. Philippe retired, too, grateful that his brother had had no desire to speak with him again. Celia waited on the steps, looking from Marguerite to Sir Richard.

"I will be fine, Celia," she said reassuringly. "I will come in to say goodnight as soon as I come upstairs."

Reluctantly Celia left them and they turned to the library, Sir Richard closing the door firmly behind them.

"I would like to speak to you about your sister," he said in a measured tone. "I think that you cannot realize the ordeal that you are subjecting her to."

Marguerite stared at him. "What do you mean by 'subjecting her to,' Sir Richard?" she asked. "Are you once again going to tell me that she does not wish to see anyone apart from the members of this household? Would you have her kept indoors?"

"Of course not!" he snapped. "But didn't you see that she was uncomfortable tonight? You were the one doing all of the talking and flirting, while she sat exposed to the glances of everyone in the theater."

"I don't think that she was in pain, Sir Richard," remarked Marguerite. "Because she is quiet does not mean that she does not enjoy hearing the badinage."

"And you would willingly subject her to the attentions of a man like Saybrook?" he demanded. "After what I told you of him?"

"I can see nothing amiss with Lord Saybrook!" she exclaimed, irritated to have his name thrown at her again. "Nothing at least except your prejudice against him! And he does not force himself upon Celia—he merely entertains us!"

"I did not see that Celia looked particularly entertained," countered Sir Richard, striking a nerve with Marguerite, for she had observed the same thing. "It seems to me, Miss Standish, that you are enjoying yourself at your sister's expense."

"You take too much upon yourself, Sir Richard!" she

exclaimed angrily. "This is none of your affair, sir! You have no right to interfere!"

He bowed. "I have your sister's best interests at heart, Miss Standish. I feel that someone should, for you clearly do not."

Infuriated by his patronizing manner and a lingering doubt about the wisdom of her course of action with Celia, she added tartly, "Well, don't worry about Lord Saybrook, Sir Richard. Perhaps if Celia does not marry him, I shall. He has described Mendassy Hall in great detail and I would greatly enjoy being mistress of it."

He stared at her for a moment, his eyes glinting with anger. "It is difficult for me to believe that you are sisters, Miss Standish. It is shocking that Miss Celia is being imposed upon by a female with so little delicacy of mind."

Then, acutely aware that his anger had led him to overstep the boundaries of good behavior, he left abruptly, not noting the shadow in the corner of the passageway. Nor did Marguerite take note of it when she left the library a moment later, wiping her eyes angrily and composing herself to look cheerful for Celia's sake.

Before retiring for the evening Philippe stopped in his mother's chamber. "Do you know, Mama, that I believe Richard may at last walk into parson's mousetrap."

Startled, she looked up and stopped Tolliver, who was performing her nightly ritual of brushing Lady Norwood's hair. "Celia?" she inquired.

Philippe nodded. "I believe that Richard may not be rushing back to Greenwood immediately."

Lady Norwood looked thoughtful, absently fingering the diamond bracelet that she had just removed and wondering how she could make this information best serve her and her son.

Meanwhile, Marguerite, brushing her own hair in her

own chamber and thinking over the situation, had reached much the same conclusion as Philippe. She could find no comfort in it, although she knew that Sir Richard would be a notable catch. But she could not think of Celia married to the grim man who so disliked her. If Celia married Sir Richard, Marguerite knew that she would never be a welcome guest in their home, and that was too bitter a thought to accept. She could not imagine what her life would be like if she were separated from Celia.

Before going to bed that night, she opened her sewing basket and patted the place where the locket was hidden, wishing that she could see the face in it that was so like her mother's. She had need of comfort.

Eleven

"Can you believe that this day has finally arrived, Celia?" asked Marguerite the next morning. The dawn had again restored to her a more balanced view of the world, and she no longer feared that her sister would marry Sir Richard. There were other choices available—Miles Randall for one—and their future lay before them.

"Thanks to the arrival of Philippe, we attend our first ball tonight," she continued. "Mind you, I did not have Bath in mind when I dreamt of this night, but I am in no mood to find fault. We will have a delightful time!"

Celia smiled, although she looked somewhat dubious. "I am sure that it will be lovely, Marguerite," she said gently. She paused for a moment, staring down at her small sandaled feet. "Mr. Randall has asked to dance with me tonight. Do you think that I will remember how to dance well enough that he won't be embarrassed, Marguerite?"

Marguerite hugged her. "You dance like an angel, Celia. You needn't be afraid. You will have a splendid time. And we will practice this afternoon so that you feel confident again."

She laid out the white dress trimmed in silver roses that she had worked on so many hours in Northaven. "You will look magnificent!" she reassured her sister. "The silver trim on the gown will accentuate the silver in your hair, and I have made roses of silver for you to thread through your curls as well."

"They are beautiful, Marguerite. Thank you." Celia picked up one of the dainty roses and held it gently on the palm of her hand, admiring it. "Have you made the hair ornament for your gown?" she asked.

"Not yet," admitted her sister. "But after we take a walk down to Milsom Street, I will have the ribbon I need to complete it."

Happily the two young ladies set forth together, always content to be in one another's company. Sir Richard's astringent comments on her treatment of Celia were still stinging, and Marguerite could not resist asking her sister a question.

"Do you think that I am pressing you, too hard to find a husband, Celia?" she inquired, watching her sister's face carefully.

Celia flushed a little, and did not answer immediately. "I am not always comfortable, Marguerite," she responded, "but you know that it's because I am foolish, I know, and too shy."

Marguerite's heart sank. Sir Richard had been right. "No, Celia, you are not foolish," she replied firmly. "I'm the one who has been foolish to make you feel that way."

"I know that I could not marry someone like Lord Saybrook, Marguerite," Celia said earnestly. "He talks in such a clever, quick way, like you do, and he is always laughing at things that I don't see, so he would never wish to marry me, and I would never be happy with him."

"Have you met anyone that you *could* be happy with, Celia?" she asked gently.

"Well, I don't know that exactly—I mean, I don't know that I could marry them—but I do like talking to both Sir Richard and Mr. Randall. They listen to me and are kind to me, so that I don't feel nervous. And they let me talk about home."

Marguerite's heart sank even farther. Sir Richard again. Well, at least Celia had a fondness for Miles Randall, too.

And she was now convinced that he was a genial and a kindly man who would treat Celia well and be happy to receive her sister in their home.

The young ladies spent a peaceful afternoon in Marguerite's chamber, Marguerite knotting scarlet ribbons to wear in her hair that evening, and Celia playing with Nipper and reading aloud from Marguerite's book of Cowper's verse. When it was time to go down to dinner, they were ready. Marguerite reflected that she had never seen Celia look more charming than she did that evening.

Dinner was a pleasant affair, for Sir Richard was not dining with them and Philippe exerted himself to be an genial host. Even Lady Norwood seemed almost amiable.

It was not until they were waiting for Lady Norwood to complete her toilette before leaving for the ball that the atmosphere changed. Philippe and Marguerite and Celia were waiting together in the drawing room when Tolliver rushed in, her face alight with a fierce excitement.

"Have you seen my lady's diamond bracelet, Mr. Norwood?" she asked feverishly.

Philippe merely looked bored. "My mother's bracelet? Of course not, Tolliver. What would I be doing with her bracelet?"

"Have you young ladies seen it?" she demanded, turning to the other two.

Marguerite and Celia shook their heads, bewildered. "I'm not sure that I have ever seen her wear a diamond bracelet," murmured Marguerite, thinking that she had seen Lady Norwood in so many pieces of jewelry that it was difficult to remember them all.

Tolliver left abruptly, and the others continued to wait patiently while the sounds of frenzied activity floated down to them from above.

"What are they doing up there?" demanded Philippe finally, giving voice to the thought that had been going through Marguerite's mind for some time. Surely the servants could search for the bracelet while they were at the ball. Lady Norwood did not have to have it in order to dance.

Finally Lady Norwood appeared and the others rose to join her.

"I am sorry that you haven't found your bracelet," began Marguerite, seeing that she was not wearing it. Before she could finish her sentence, however, the butler entered, carrying the bracelet.

"Oh, Stephens, how grateful I am!" exclaimed Lady Norwood. "Where did you find it?"

Stephens glanced at the young ladies diffidently, and said in a low voice, "One of the maids found it on the dressing table of the younger Miss Standish," he replied, indicating Celia with a nod of his head.

Marguerite heard herself gasp and saw Celia's eyes fill with tears as she shook her head. "How could that be?" asked Celia breathlessly. "I have never even seen the bracelet before."

Philippe and Lady Norwood both looked shocked. "I am certain that there must be some mistake," began Philippe, and Marguerite echoed his sentiment, but the butler shook his head.

"The maid is quite positive about where she found it," he responded.

"And I saw it, too," added Tolliver from the doorway where she stood, hovering over the scene like one of Macbeth's weird sisters. "Allow me, my lady," she said to Lady Norwood, bending over her to fasten the clasp of the bracelet.

"We had best be on our way," said Lady Norwood coolly, removing herself to a slight distance from her guests. "We are already late."

Marguerite looked at her sister's tearstained face and reluctantly shook her head. "I don't believe that we should go, Lady Norwood," she said slowly. "I am afraid that this has upset Celia too much for her to be able to enjoy the evening."

"I am a trifle distressed myself," observed Lady Norwood tartly, "but one must do what one must do, and attending tonight is something of a duty for me. I am expected."

Their goodbyes from Lady Norwood and Philippe were decidedly chilly, and Marguerite wondered if they seriously thought that she and Celia were capable of such ungrateful behavior as stealing a piece of jewelry. Then she remembered the locket secreted in her basket and flushed.

She could not allow herself to appear distressed, however. She accompanied Celia to her chamber, maintaining a cheerful chatter about what they would do the following day, and soothing Celia accordingly. It was not until Celia was almost asleep that a maid scratched at the door to announce the presence of Sir Richard in the drawing room.

"Tell him I am grateful that he has come, Marguerite, but I don't wish to go down to see him. You don't think that he will be angry, do you?" asked Celia, rising sleepily from her pillow.

"Of course not, Celia. I will tell him that you were just drifting off to sleep."

When she entered the drawing room, she saw with some relief that he was alone. She would not need to face Lady Norwood or Philippe again that night.

"What has happened here tonight, Miss Standish?" he demanded.

Marguerite gave him a brief account of the troubles of the evening, and watched with pleasure as his face darkened. At least he was not going to take this insult to them lightly.

"I knew that something was amiss when I saw them enter without you tonight," he explained briefly. "I cannot believe that Celia has been placed in such a situation. Any fool would know that *she* would not be capable of doing such a thing!"

Marguerite's back grew straighter and her lips thinner as she listened to him defend Celia. "I see, sir, that you feel no such outrage on my part," she remarked sharply. "I take that to mean that you could believe that *I* had taken the bracelet?"

"Of course not, Miss Standish!" he snapped. "No one has accused you, although you *have* already shown your interest in jewelry and in making the most of your opportunities."

Marguerite rose abruptly and marched to the door, not turning back when she heard him call her name. She had had to endure quite enough for one day and she wanted no more of him.

She stopped in Celia's room to be certain that she was now deeply asleep and then retired to the safety of her own room. On the pillow she caught a glimpse of something unfamiliar. It was another note: this one simply said *I warned you.*

Angrily she unpinned it, folded it tightly, and slipped it into her bodice. This note she would keep on her person— and she would show it to Lady Norwood at the first possible opportunity. She would like very much to know who had been responsible for the latest note, for undoubtedly it was also the person responsible for Celia's disaster that evening. Someone was creating problems for them and taking a malicious pleasure in their trouble. She very much hoped that she would soon be able to confront that individual.

Taking a fresh piece of paper, she wrote in bold, black letters, *I know who you are.* Then she slipped it inside the same book of poetry in her lap desk where she had hidden the first one. The intruder had found it there one time, and Marguerite was certain that her room would be searched again.

Twelve

The next morning Marguerite went immediately to Lady Norwood's chamber, knowing that lady was still in bed. She had waited until she had seen Tolliver go downstairs so that she would not have to confront the dragon in order to be allowed into the room. There was at first no response, but finally she heard Lady Norwood's voice, sleepily indignant.

She entered the room quickly and made certain that the door was firmly closed behind her.

"Marguerite!" exclaimed Lady Norwood crossly from her pillow. "Whatever do you want at this ungodly hour?"

"It is already nine o'clock, Lady Norwood," she replied briskly, "and I must speak to you before the day grows any older." She drew back the curtains and her hostess groaned at the sudden influx of light, pulling the covers over her eyes.

"What are you doing, you thoughtless girl?" demanded Lady Norwood crossly. "You know that I was out until all hours last night and that I'm not strong. Why are you disturbing me so early in the day?"

Marguerite forced herself to look regretful—which was difficult as she looked at the petulant expression before her—and managed to reply in a voice filled with compunction. "I beg your pardon, Lady Norwood, but something most serious has occurred, and I knew that, as mistress of the house, you would wish to know of it immediately."

Lady Norwood struggled to sit upright, her eyes suddenly wide and her cap askew. "What is it?" she asked, her voice suddenly tense. "Has something happened to Philippe?"

"No, of course not, Lady Norwood. I didn't mean to frighten you," she apologized. "It is something concerning my sister and me and someone else in your household."

The lady's sudden change in expression informed Marguerite that she could bear this sort of news much more calmly, and she took a moment to fluff the pillows behind her and to adjust her cap.

"What is it then?" she asked in irritation. "Surely it is something that could have waited until later in the day."

Marguerite shook her head, taking the note from her pocket and unfolding it. "I don't think so," she responded, extending the note to her. "It cost me a sleepless night after I found it on my pillow yesterday evening, and I thought that you would wish to take immediate steps to find the author of this threatening note."

Lady Norwood smoothed the note and lay it on the counterpane, studying it. "What sort of foolishness is this? 'I warned you.' What on earth does that mean? Warned you about what?" she demanded.

"I'm not certain what I am being warned of, Lady Norwood," responded Marguerite gravely. "But this was placed on my pillow last night, and it was certainly placed there by someone within this household, not a stranger that came in off the street."

"Surely this is not something you take seriously, Marguerite," Lady Norwood said pettishly, pushing the slip of paper aside.

"And why should I not take it seriously, ma'am?" she asked in surprise, refolding the note and putting it away. "When someone sneaks into my chamber and leaves a threatening note on my pillow, I am inclined to take it personally."

"Then you are unforgivably foolish," replied Lady Norwood lightly, picking up her mirror and delicately patting a scented cream from a small gold jar onto the skin about her eyes. "Warned you about what, after all? It is all so melodramatic—like something out of one of the gothic novels that are all the rage now. And I know that you read a great deal, Marguerite. Have you considered that your reading may be having too great an influence upon you?"

Marguerite stared at her in astonishment. "What has my reading to say to anything, ma'am? Are you suggesting that I put the note on my own pillow?"

"No, of course not," said Lady Norwood hastily. "Merely that you are regarding this as a weighty matter when it was probably nothing more than a thoughtless joke. Probably the person who did it regrets it already."

"The person who did it, ma'am, had already sent me one warning note before I even left Northaven to come to your home."

Lady Norwood looked up sharply, her attention fully engaged for the moment. "You have received another note? What did it say?" she inquired.

Marguerite nodded. "It warned us not to go to Norwood House because it was a dangerous place for us. And it ended with the words *Remember what happened to your mother.*"

Lady Norwood stared at her for a moment, and then, shrugging, returned to her mirror and the cream. "You see what I mean, my dear?" she said casually. "That is the stuff theatricals are made of. Have you that note with you?"

Marguerite shook her head reluctantly. "I had it in my lap desk when I first came here," she said slowly, "but it disappeared after my room was searched."

This time Lady Norwood did stop her beauty routine completely, putting down her mirror and cream and staring at her. "Are you mad, girl? Do you mean to say that you think someone searched your room and took something from your lap desk?"

Marguerite nodded miserably. She knew precisely how farfetched it all sounded. "It is true, Lady Norwood."

Lady Norwood lay back on her pillows and studied her for a moment. "You know, my dear," she said, her voice suddenly pleasant and soothing, "I believe that what you need is to get out more than you have been. I fear that my keeping you too close to home has made you fanciful. I know that you are accustomed to more exercise, and that you have longed to get out more. I shall do something about that."

"I am very grateful, Lady Norwood, but that does not take care of the matter of the notes—"

Lady Norwood waved her hand, cutting her off. "Nonsense! The notes are a trifling matter, not worth troubling yourself over."

"But the matter of your diamond bracelet, Lady Norwood—that was not a trifling matter," Marguerite reminded her. "The first note warned us of trouble if we came to you, and this note," and here she waved last night's note in the air, "made me feel that the matter of the bracelet might have been planned by someone."

"Planned?" demanded Lady Norwood. "Why should anyone wish to harm the two of you?"

This, of course, was the sticking point. Why *should* anyone—except perhaps Tolliver—wish to harm them? Reluctantly, Marguerite said, "Jealousy, perhaps?"

Lady Norwood's laughter rang through the room. "Jealousy! I fear that you are feverish, Marguerite. Who would be jealous of you here? Philippe? Myself? Scarcely, my dear." And she sank back onto her pillows, almost overcome by merriment at the thought.

Marguerite interrupted her laughter hesitantly. "No, of course not either of you, ma'am. But I had wondered about Tolliver—"

"Tolliver!" exclaimed Lady Norwood, her eyes wide. "So now even my poor Tolliver is to be suspected of sending crank notes?" She dismissed the thought with a wave of her hand and continued before Marguerite could explain further. "I can see that I must certainly do something about giving you more to think about. There is a concert tonight at the Assembly Rooms, and we shall most assuredly attend it. It may be a wretched program, but it will at least get us out. I believe that I shall plan a program of activities that will give you something more to dwell upon than mysterious notes."

"That is very kind of you, ma'am," replied Marguerite, pleased to hear of the change in schedule, for she *was* eager to go out more frequently, "still, it does not explain—"

Lady Norwood held up her hand. "Enough, Marguerite! You will make me quite as mad as you are, if you continue. We will begin your cure immediately. Have Stephens order the carriage round for an early morning drive to Widcombe and back to restore your nerves, then have the driver set you down at Bath Street to run an errand for me there. I shall send Tolliver over to your room with the particulars."

Marguerite stared at her, quite astonished by this sudden interest in their welfare. "That would be delightful," she responded, thinking of how much Celia would enjoy the drive, but—"

"There is no but about it," replied Lady Norwood briskly. "Just do as I have bid you. You and Celia be ready as quickly as possible and you can begin to shake from your mind the cobwebs that allow you to think such fearfully gothic thoughts."

Marguerite managed a weak laugh. "Perhaps you are right, ma'am," she said, tucking the note away in her pocket. She was quite certain that Lady Norwood was wrong, but she had no way at all to prove it.

"Of course I am!" exclaimed that lady confidently. "Now take yourself to your room and prepare for your day. This afternoon I shall have Madame Stacey come to us here to fashion some new gowns for you and Celia. If you are to have a busier social schedule, you must have an ample wardrobe."

Thoroughly astonished now, Marguerite managed to stammer, "That is most kind of you, ma'am," before retreating to the passageway.

Once outside she stood and stared at Lady Norwood's door. What on earth was happening, she wondered. She could think of no satisfactory explanation for her hostess's behavior, unless she had simply undergone a change of heart after realizing the sort of treatment her guests had been subjected to.

Patting the note in her pocket, she started toward Celia's room to share the good news with her. Surely this would give her thoughts a more positive turn and keep her from sitting inside fretting about the bracelet.

Thirteen

One glance at Celia's face was enough to assure Marguerite that she had been right in accepting Lady Norwood's offer of a drive. The lavender shadows under her eyes, which had begun to fade during the past days, were now great smudges, and the light was gone from her eyes.

"Come now, Celia," she exclaimed. "Put on your blue walking dress and your hat and prepare for a delightful drive."

Celia looked puzzled. "A drive? Is Sir Richard taking us out then?"

"Sir Richard is not taking us anywhere, Celia." She was unreasonably annoyed by her sister's belief that Sir Richard would be the only one interested in their welfare. It was troubling that Celia thought so highly of a man who all too clearly agreed with her opinion.

"Lady Norwood has sent for her own carriage and we are to take a drive to Widcombe," she continued in a more pleasant tone. "You know that you have heard everyone speak of how charming a village that is."

Celia's face brightened perceptibly at the news. "Lady Norwood is sending us in her carriage?" she asked hopefully. "Does that mean that she does not believe that I stole her bracelet?"

"Well, of course she does not, dear goose. Who could believe such a thing of you?" She lowered her voice and glanced toward the door. "I believe that it was Tolliver

who placed it on your dressing table. She has been deathly
jealous of you from the first day we arrived."

Celia's eyes widened. "Do you mean that Tolliver might
have placed it there deliberately?" she asked in distress.
"Surely she would not have done such a cruel thing, Marguerite!"

Marguerite patted her shoulder comfortingly. "You
know that everyone does not think about things as you
do, Celia. Tolliver probably views you as a threat, someone who might take her place with Lady Norwood."

"But I could not do that! I haven't the ability to look
after her as Tolliver does."

"I expect that Tolliver realizes that—but that does not
make her any less jealous of the attention and affection
that Lady Norwood has shown you. After all, she has been
serving her for years, and in a few days you appear to
have taken all of that from her."

Marguerite was sorry that she had mentioned the matter
of Tolliver, for Celia's thoughts had now taken another
unhappy turn, and she was distressed with herself for having caused Tolliver pain. Once again Marguerite reflected
that Papa's teachings had taken far too firm a hold on
Celia's kind nature. She readily assumed guilt that was
not hers to carry. She thought for a moment of showing
Celia the notes so that she would feel less pity for Tolliver,
but then decided that doing so would simply make Celia
feel more guilty than ever. She would doubtless feel responsible for forcing Tolliver to take such desperate measures. The thing to do was to get Celia out of the house
as soon as possible and divert her thoughts in other, more
productive directions.

Before they could leave, however, Stephens informed
them that Lord Saybrook had called and was awaiting
them in the drawing room.

"Lord Saybrook!" exclaimed Marguerite in

astonishment. "Why would he be calling upon us so early in the day?"

"I am sure that I don't know the answer to that, miss," replied Stephens stiffly, obviously irritated by Lord Say brook's failure to observe the unwritten code of society One did not pay calls until the afternoon, though the call were, oddly enough, then called "morning calls." "I in formed him that you were about to step out, but he in sisted that I inform you that he is here and that he need to have a word with you before you leave."

"Thank you, Stephens," Marguerite replied. "I will be down in just a moment."

"I don't want to see him, Marguerite," said Celia afte the door closed behind Stephens. "He probably knows th story of the bracelet—I should imagine everyone at th ball last night knows the story! How shall I ever be able to face any of them?"

"Nonsense," replied Marguerite firmly. "You can cer tainly face one or all of them, because you know that you did nothing wrong. How can anyone accuse you with no proof?"

"You know how people gossip," replied her sister with an uncharacteristic bitterness. "And that they are usually all too happy to believe the worst of anyone. I should imagine my story was a great hit last night."

Marguerite knew that she was right and was troubled by her sister's new bleakness. She was certain that Lord Saybrook would not have called to bring them any un pleasant news, however, and so she encouraged Celia to lift her chin and accompany her downstairs.

When the two young ladies entered the drawing room they were astonished to see that Lord Saybrook was bearing a huge bouquet for each of them.

"How very kind of you!" exclaimed Marguerite sincerely, for the blossoms were beautiful.

"They are from my own greenhouses," said Saybrook

proudly. "I sent to Mendassy for them early this morning, so they are as fresh and springlike as though they had been plucked from your mother's garden."

He turned to Celia and bowed. "You see that I have been eavesdropping on your conversations with young Randall, Miss Standish."

"Thank you, Lord Saybrook," responded Celia in a low voice, but with an unaccustomed smile. "You are very thoughtful."

"I can only feel that I have done them an unkindness by bringing them here where they may be compared with the beauty of you and your sister, dear lady," responded Saybrook, never one to allow the opportunity to pay a fulsome compliment slip by.

The pleasantry unfortunately covered Celia with her customary confusion, and she lapsed into silence while the other two talked. Upon hearing that they were about to drive out to Widcombe, he insisted that he be allowed to accompany them and that they take his own carriage. Marguerite at first demurred, but finally gave way when he reminded her that they would really wish to walk most of the way, and would only want the carriage for their shopping errands.

"So do allow me to be your guide, Miss Standish," he said gently. "It will be a pleasure to show you the way. There is a raised narrow footpath for much of the walk, and the prospect is quite beautiful."

Charmed by the idea of a country walk instead of a drive, even Celia gave way to his wishes, and the rest of the morning was spent in a cheerful ramble, admiring the church and the manor at Widcombe to their hearts' content.

"You will have to visit me at Mendassy," said Lord Saybrook, listening to their admiring comments about the beauty of the countryside. "I am very prejudiced, I know, but I think that there are few places as lovely."

"We would love to, Lord Saybrook," replied Marguerite,

and even Celia nodded, cheered by the thought of yet another country outing.

When they at last were set down at Bath Street to execute their errands for Lady Norwood, they encountered almost immediately Mrs. Pribble and Mrs. Scott, two ladies that they had met in the Pump Room. Although the ladies responded to Marguerite's greeting, their manner was decidedly stiff and cool.

As they walked away, Celia clasped Marguerite's arm. "They have heard the story of the bracelet," she whispered frantically. "That is why they behaved in such an odd manner."

"Nonsense!" responded Marguerite firmly, although she knew with a sinking certainty that Celia was right and that this was a far more serious matter than she had guessed. If Lady Norwood were treating the bracelet episode so lightly today, why would she have made the story known last night? And she must have done so—or perhaps Philippe had. Or perhaps the gossip of the servants had spread the story since few things traveled more rapidly.

She glanced at Lord Saybrook, but he appeared to have noticed nothing. Indeed, he seemed deeply occupied with his own thoughts, but he emerged from them abruptly, turning to Celia and Marguerite and bowing.

"Forgive me, ladies, if I abandon you for a moment. I have just remembered a purchase that I must make. I will rejoin you in a very few minutes at Jarrod's. That is your last stop, is it not?"

Marguerite nodded silently and he hurried away.

"He knows the story, too," observed Celia bleakly. "And he has decided that it will not improve his credit to be seen with us. I cannot say that I blame him, however."

"As always, Celia, you are a kinder person than I am," said Marguerite. "If I were certain that were true, I would be furious with him for abandoning us because he sees that we are now socially unacceptable."

She considered the matter for a moment, then added more reasonably, "After all, Lord Saybrook is not likely to be impressed by the actions of Mrs. Pribble and Mrs. Scott. Perhaps he was being truthful and will join us shortly."

Having completed two of their errands for Lady Norwood, the girls continued down Bath Street toward Jarrod's. The door to Ripton's, a small confectionery, opened, and Sir Devon Radcliffe and his daughter Hester, two others known to them from the Pump Room, emerged onto the pavement. Seeing Celia and Marguerite, they afforded them the briefest of bows and continued on their way without speaking.

"You can see that it is just as I said it would be, Marguerite," said Celia in a low voice. "Let us return home immediately before anyone else has the opportunity to cut us. I cannot bear any more of this."

"There is one errand that we must complete for Lady Norwood, and then we will go directly back to the Crescent," Marguerite assured her. "While I am looking for what she needs, Celia, I would like for you to match this ribbon for me." She handed Celia a scarlet ribbon, hoping that giving her something to do would help to occupy her mind.

Once inside Jarrod's, Celia set about matching the ribbon and, completing her charge before her sister, paid for it and gazed idly about the shop. In the meantime, Marguerite had removed from her reticule the piece of lace that she was trying to match for Lady Norwood, who had caught her dress the evening before and torn the trim. Having at last found a satisfactory match, she paid for it and the two girls stepped onto the pavement carrying their parcels.

No sooner had they done so than the pretty young clerk from Jarrod's came running after them, shouting, "Stop, thief!" The girls stopped and looked about them in bewilderment, wondering what could have happened in the brief period of time since they had left the shop. The clerk, however, ran directly to Celia and snatched the parcel from her hands.

Before Marguerite could protest such outrageous behavior, the clerk had ripped it open, exposing not only the scarlet ribbons that Celia had purchased, but also a card of costly lace.

"But I didn't purchase that!" exclaimed Celia, horrified.

"I should say that you did not, miss," said the owner of the shop grimly. He had apparently followed the clerk onto the pavement, and he sternly took Celia's arm and guided her back into the shop. "You were charged for the ribbons only, but it seems that you slipped something else into the packet."

"She did no such thing!" protested Marguerite, following them. "Your clerk must have made a mistake. I'm certain that there is a reasonable explanation for this."

"I believe so myself, miss," said the owner in clipped tones. "And so I will tell the magistrate when I bring this young lady up on charges."

Marguerite and Celia stood transfixed at his words. They knew that the heaviest punishment possible for such an offense was death, the lightest, transportation.

"You cannot do such a thing!" exclaimed Marguerite. "My sister is guilty of nothing!"

"She certainly is and I shall see to it that she pays for her misdeeds."

"Nonsense!" said a voice sharply. "You will do no such thing, sir! I was a witness to this whole unsavory matter. I was waiting by the front door of your shop and I watched the young woman in your employ place that card of lace in this young lady's parcel. Should you bring charges against her, I would most certainly file counter-charges against your clerk! And you will unhand that young lady!"

"And who, may I ask, are you, sir?" inquired the owner of the shop with an air of bravado, relinquishing his grip on Celia's elbow and turning to stare at the gentleman who had confronted him.

"Oh, thank you, Lord Saybrook!" sobbed Celia, clinging to her sister. "I am so grateful that you saw it all!"

The proprietor had grown noticeably pale during this speech. "Lord Saybrook?" he stammered, recognizing the name of one of the wealthiest men in the region. "Of Mendassy Hall?" Not waiting for confirmation of this fact, he tried to regain his composure and said grandly, "But of course such measures will not be needed. It is assuredly all a misunderstanding."

He turned to the clerk, who was staring at him in bewilderment, and snatched Celia's parcel from her hands. "Imbecile!" he hissed. "How could you mistreat one of our customers in such a manner?"

He hastily retied the parcel and handed it to Celia, begging her to accept the lace as an indication of his distress over the unfortunate incident. Marguerite returned the lace firmly, ignoring his protests as he bowed them to the door, apologizing profusely.

Lord Saybrook shepherded them to a nearby tea shop and ordered tea and buns to calm them while he inquired into the situation. In the comforting dimness of the tiny, low-raftered room, filled with the homey smell of baking bread, Celia began to regain her composure.

"I am so grateful that you were a witness to what happened, Lord Saybrook," she said, her voice still shaking. "I cannot thank you enough for taking my part." She shuddered. "Otherwise, that man would at this moment have me in front of the magistrate and they would soon be taking me away to jail."

"Yes, Lord Saybrook," said Marguerite briskly, hoping that her matter-of-fact tone would help to calm her sister, "we have much to thank you for. You were very good to take our part."

"Nonsense!" he replied, his dark eyes drawn together.

"The man is a rascal, and I may have him up on charges for what he has attempted to do. What I wish to know is why he would have done such a thing. How would it profit him to accuse Miss Celia?"

Marguerite, who had not had time to consider this aspect of the matter, nodded her head slowly. "That is peculiar," she agreed. "We are penniless, so he cannot have hoped that we would attempt to bribe him to avoid the charges. What other reason could he have had for such behavior?"

She stirred her tea thoughtfully, and the other two considered the matter in silence. Finally Lord Saybrook turned to Celia. "Perhaps it would help, ma'am," he said gently, "if you could tell us exactly what happened. If we put that together with what your sister and I saw, we may be able to piece together the puzzle."

To Marguerite's surprise, Celia responded, giving him as precise an account as she could, her voice still shaking a little. Marguerite reflected that this was the most Celia had had to say to Lord Saybrook since they had met him. He listened in silence, offering an occasional encouraging nod.

"And I wish to say again that I am most grateful that you appeared when you did, Lord Saybrook," she said shyly, as she ended her account of the episode. "Marguerite and I had feared that you might have decided to have nothing to do with us since there was the accident of the bracelet last night. We were afraid that when you saw others cutting us, you might not wish for our acquaintance either."

Lord Saybrook looked sharply at Marguerite, who had the grace to blush. "You have proved us wrong, Lord Saybrook. I apologize for misjudging you," she said contritely.

He bowed in acknowledgment of her apology, and the afternoon ended more pleasantly than they would have believed possible, as he guided the conversation to more agreeable subjects, like the prospect of a party at Mendassy.

After he had seen them to their door in the Crescent,

he sat for a few moments in his carriage, considering the events of the past two days. Two such "accidents" in twenty-four hours—and he had heard all about the diamond bracelet at the ball last night—constituted too great a coincidence for his taste. It was possible, of course, that the clerk had been merely trying to blackmail Celia for whatever pocket money she could extract—but there could be more to it than that. It was time that he talked to Sir Richard Norwood about the two young ladies.

That very afternoon found Lord Saybrook at the White Hart Hotel, inquiring for Sir Richard, whom he located in the taproom. He knew how much Sir Richard disliked him and how distasteful it would be to him to have to receive him and to discuss personal matters with him—so Lord Saybrook was prepared to enjoy their meeting thoroughly.

"Saybrook," said Sir Richard unenthusiastically. "You were asking for me?"

Saybrook nodded. "I think that we had best retire to a more private place to talk, however, Norwood. This concerns matters that you won't wish to have bandied about in public."

Raising his eyebrows almost to his hairline, Sir Richard rose from his seat and led him to his own sitting room. Pouring a glass of brandy, he handed it to his guest and said unencouragingly, "So tell me, Saybrook—what is weighing so heavily upon you that you must seek me out to discuss it?"

"The two young ladies visiting Lady Norwood are, I think, in some danger," replied his guest, sipping the brandy in a meditative manner.

Sir Richard's dark brows snapped together. "In danger?" he said sharply. "What are you talking about, Saybrook?"

"I'm talking about the fact that Miss Celia Standish was accused of the theft of a diamond bracelet just last night—" he began, but Sir Richard broke in.

"Yes, I am aware of that incident, Saybrook," he said,

his color heightened. "Although there was never any question of her being accused of theft. It was, I think, a simple misunderstanding—and certainly not, I think, a danger."

"I am certain that it was a misunderstanding," responded Saybrook dryly, "but whether or not it was a simple misunderstanding, completely lacking in danger, is another question. You realize that I am not the only one who is aware of last night's incident?"

Sir Richard's color darkened further. "Yes," he said, nodding briefly. "I know that it was talked of."

"Not just talked of in a casual manner by a few people," corrected Saybrook gently. "Everyone present at the ball heard the story, and no one heard that the accusation of theft was a misunderstanding. Everyone who was there is still laboring under the misapprehension that Miss Celia was indeed accused of theft."

Sir Richard brought down his fist on the table, wishing that he had his stepmother and Philippe close enough at hand to express his feelings. He was keenly aware that one, or possibly both, of them had been responsible for Celia's public embarrassment. And now he was having to hear of it from a man such as Saybrook.

"I was with the young ladies today on Bath Street when they were cut several times by acquaintances of yours," continued Lord Saybrook. "It would have been a demoralizing experience for anyone, but particularly so for young ladies who are unaccustomed to our pleasant city manners."

Sir Richard nodded curtly. "I will do what I can to remedy the situation, Saybrook. But this still does not explain what you meant by the remark about their being in danger. Such an accusation is decidedly demoralizing, but not necessarily dangerous—except to the reputation."

Briefly Lord Saybrook apprised him of the episode at Jarrod's. "And so, as you can see, Norwood," he concluded, "it strikes me as very odd indeed that two such accidents could occur within twenty-four hours of one another. I am suspicious by nature, and this whole business reeks of deceit."

Sir Richard nodded slowly, unwilling to agree with Saybrook about anything, but he was just as certain as that gentleman that these were not coincidences. Someone had planned for Celia to be humiliated publicly, and judging by this afternoon, perhaps even to be placed in prison. He was mystified. There seemed to be no one who would have anything to gain from such an action.

"Do you have a suggestion then, Saybrook?" he inquired reluctantly, able to think of none of his own.

"Indeed I do, Sir Richard," he responded, bowing briefly. "We must show people that the Standish ladies are accepted by us and that there is no hint of scandal attached to them."

"How would you suggest that we do that?" he asked dryly, certain that Saybrook had already worked out a plan.

"It is a very simple matter," Saybrook responded. "I am well received in Bath—you must admit the truth of that, Norwood, although I know that you deplore it," he added, regarding Sir Richard's dark expression with a winning smile, enjoying his discomfiture.

"And so," he continued, "I will invite the young ladies—and the other members of your family of course—to be my guests of honor for a party at Mendassy. It will be a very fine affair that attracts a great deal of attention—we will leave on flowered barges and make our way down to Mendassy, where our musicians will serenade us while we dance and dine *al fresco.* Everyone will see that they are indeed to be received and respected. When we all return to Bath, they will be invited everywhere. Their success will be a *fait accompli.*"

Much as it galled Sir Richard to do so, he could see that he had no choice but to graciously thank Saybrook for his interest and his suggestion—for he was quite in agreement that something was seriously amiss in the affairs of the Standish ladies. He realized also that it was his responsibility to set things right if it could possibly be done. They were, after all, guests of his family, and he could not have their reputations dragged through the mud. Added to that was the fact that he had grown quite fond of Celia and, whatever he might think of her sister, she at least did not deserve to be treated as poorly as this.

The bitterest part of the whole business was that he was not solving the problem himself, but it was foolish to deny that Saybrook, with all of the glory of Mendassy behind him, was not a godsend. He was forced to admit to himself, too, that he had overreacted when he had seen Saybrook with Marguerite and Celia. He reflected that it would be more difficult still to admit it to the elder Miss Standish when he lent his support to the Mendassy outing. Humble pie was never a dish that he favored.

Sir Richard called on the ladies just before dinner that evening, and his reception was just as he had imagined it would be.

"Well, Richard, really!" exclaimed Lady Norwood when he entered the drawing room. "You might have let me know that you were coming for dinner. You know how easily Cook gets upset and there are precisely enough guinea-fowls for each of us. How very like you to throw everything off like this."

"He may have mine, ma'am," Celia assured her. "I am not particularly hungry tonight. We had Bath buns and tea rather late and I'm afraid that it spoiled my appetite."

Sir Richard bowed to her and smiled. "That is very gracious of you, Celia, but I am not staying for dinner. I am meeting friends very shortly."

"Well, why did you not say so immediately?" demanded Lady Norwood, not appearing particularly pleased that her problem with the cook and the guinea-fowls had been so easily resolved. "You were always the most aggravating, inconsiderate boy and you have not changed a whit now that you are a man!"

"I take pride in my consistency, ma'am," he assured her blandly. "I merely stopped by to let you know that I will not be returning to Greenwood Park immediately, as I had planned. I shall be spending at least a fortnight here in Bath."

"Will you really?" asked his stepmother, with a distinct lack of enthusiasm. "We are delighted to hear it, Richard."

"What brought about this change of heart?" inquired Philippe, who also sounded less than pleased by this turn of events. Marguerite, who was wondering the same thing, listened intently.

Sir Richard shrugged noncommittally. "A few business matters have turned out to be knottier than I had at first thought them."

"Indeed?" remarked his brother, and waited, but there was no other comment forthcoming on the subject.

Instead, Sir Richard turned to Celia and Marguerite. "I know that it is late notice, but I had hoped that you might join me at the theater for *Macbeth* tonight. I have a box reserved." He glanced at the startled expressions of Lady Norwood and Philippe. "I would be delighted, of course, if you could join me as well."

"Macbeth?" said Philippe incredulously. "I think not, thank you, dear brother. I have other plans for the evening."

"Ma'am?" he inquired, looking at his stepmother.

Lady Norwood held her hand to her forehead. "I am still not feeling at all the thing, Richard. My poor nerves have been shattered by the events of the day."

She glanced at Celia and Marguerite. "Who would have thought that having a pair of young girls would bring such excitement into our lives? I think it might be best if we all stayed at home where—one would think—unexpected things are less likely to happen."

Celia flushed at this reference to her two grim experiences, while Marguerite merely looked angry.

"I trust," said Sir Richard, "that I shall have the honor of escorting the two of you to the theater tonight." He was sure that it would do the ladies no harm to be seen in his company that evening. In that way, the rest of Bath society would see that they were not to be treated as social lepers. Lord Saybrook might begin his grandiose plans for the Mendassy extravanganza, but Sir Richard felt that he himself must do something immediate and practical.

"Indeed you shall, Sir Richard," replied Marguerite crisply. "I think that is precisely what we need."

As it turned out, it was the very tonic that Marguerite had hoped for. The evening was an unqualified success, for Celia enjoyed the rich crimson and gold of the theater and the lovely gowns of the ladies. They had an excellent view from their box, which was in the first tier, and they were free to watch both the play and the audience at their leisure.

The production of *Macbeth* was a lively one, complete with a rather ridiculous dance of the weird sisters that was peculiar to the Bath stage. Sir Richard, once again as agreeable a host as he had been on their first outing in Bath, informed them that so illustrious an actor as John Philip Kemble had requested its removal from the play because its foolishness distracted from the remainder of the action; the management had agreed, but the audiences had insisted upon its reinstitution—and so it had remained a part of every performance of *Macbeth*.

Marguerite did not mind that the dance robbed the play of something of its dignity; she reveled in every moment of it, and her pleasure was clear to Sir Richard, who marveled that it took so little to please her. Celia, noticing his glance and correctly interpreting his thoughts, said in a low voice, "Marguerite has always longed to live in a city so that she can attend the theater and the libraries and see more of people than she did in Northaven. She always felt as though she were buried there."

They resumed their conversation during the first interval while Marguerite was absent for a few moments.

"And so your sister has always longed for a more lively existence than Northaven had to offer?" he inquired, hoping that she would enlarge upon the subject for him. It was, of course, exactly the attitude he would have expected from Marguerite.

"Yes," Celia replied gently. "I have always felt guilty for keeping her there."

"For keeping her there?" asked Sir Richard, frowning. "How did you keep her there, Miss Celia?"

"After Mama died, she would not leave home because she didn't want me to be alone with only Papa to look after me. She could have married or Mrs. Ruscombe would have sent her away to school—which was what she really wanted to do—but she wouldn't accept any of the offers."

"Indeed?" asked Sir Richard. "Would it be indiscreet if I asked why she didn't wish to leave you with only your father at home?"

Celia flushed and stared down at her hands, folded gracefully in her lap. "It seems disloyal to Papa, but—he was not a very happy man, you see. It was Mama who always made life pleasant at home, and when she died, Marguerite took that upon herself. She taught me my lessons and helped me to enjoy each day there. She was afraid that life would be too gloomy for me if I were left alone."

Here she looked up earnestly at Sir Richard. "And, even though it is unkind to say, Sir Richard—she was right. I would have been lost if she had left me. I would be lost if she left me today—and she has promised that she won't do so. If I choose not to marry, she will teach at a young ladies' seminary and I will keep house for her."

"That scarcely sounds like the lively life that your sister

has been looking forward to," he responded doubtfully. He had been quite sure that Marguerite was looking forward to elegant clothes and a constant round of social activities once Celia had married.

"Marguerite would be happy," Celia replied confidently. "She would be busy, and she would have her books and theater. Those are the things that she has always longed for. It is for me that she has wanted more. She is afraid, I think, that if I were to marry someone like Vincent Beezley—"

"Vincent Beezley!" he exclaimed, his interest caught by the name. "Forgive me for interrupting, but do tell me about Mr. Beezley."

Celia laughed. "He wished to marry me, but he has buried two of his wives, and Marguerite told him that I was not going to be the third. He has six terrible children and he thought that I could come and take care of them for him."

Sir Richard shuddered. "Your sister sent him about his business, did she?"

Celia nodded, smiling. "Marguerite is very good at expressing herself. I think that she was afraid, though, that in Northaven the only men I would have the opportunity to marry would be like Mr. Beezley, and she told me that she had enough of her relatives in the churchyard."

Sir Richard nodded, beginning to perceive that Marguerite's motives might have been somewhat different from those that he had first attributed to her.

At this point Marguerite reentered the box, in the company of Lord Saybrook and Miles Randall.

"Celia!" she exclaimed, her face wreathed in smiles. "We are invited to attend a party at Mendassy next week. Lord Saybrook is having barges carry us down the river to his estate and there will be musicians playing for us and flowers and refreshments. It sounds delightful!"

Lord Saybrook bowed. "I am pleased that it sounds agreeable, Miss Standish. I would like to make a slight correction in what you just said, however. You are not merely invited—you two ladies are my guests of honor. I shall be delighted to be able to show you my beloved home."

Celia smiled at him and held out her hand. "That is very kind of you, Lord Saybrook. I know why you are doing it—for much the same reason that Sir Richard escorted us to the theater tonight."

Marguerite stared at her in astonishment. Never would she have expected her sister to have so much to say for herself—nor would she have believed that Celia was fully alive to what these two gentlemen were doing to help her unhappy situation.

Marguerite had not particularly longed for Sir Richard's company, but she had appreciated what he was trying to do for Celia. It had not crossed her mind, however, that Celia might also realize and appreciate it. It occurred to her that she could have seriously underestimated her sister. It occurred to her, too, less comfortably, that Sir Richard might well be responsible for some of the changes she had noted in Celia. She was forced to concede that there might be more to him than met the eye.

"I hope that you will allow me to ride on the same barge with you, Miss Celia," said Miles Randall, bending over her hand.

She smiled up at him. "That would be lovely, Mr. Randall," she replied smoothly.

Marguerite gave a small sigh of pleasure as the next act of the play began. Things were looking much better than she would have believed possible a few short hours ago.

As Marguerite made herself comfortable in her chair, she was unaware that Sir Richard was studying her. It was possible, he admitted to himself, that he had been too hasty in his judgment of the elder Miss Standish. Admiring her dark lashes and the curve of her cheek, he realized that he was pleased to have been so mistaken. Apologizing could be a very pleasant matter.

Fourteen

The next few days were filled with activities. Lady Norwood made good her promise of having a dressmaker provide some new gowns for her guests, and she appeared to have forgotten—at least for the moment—that she was an invalid. They attended a round of breakfasts, card parties, assembly balls and concerts, plays and private parties. The gentlemen vied to escort them, and Lady Norwood, who chose to regard it all as a tribute to her, never tired of saying that it looked as though they were a royal entourage. Fortunately, her temper held and their days were sunny, preventing any further scandalmongering.

Sir Richard had watched for an opportunity to have a private word with Marguerite, but such moments seemed elusive. Wherever Marguerite was, Lord Saybrook seemed to be also. So much so, in fact, that Sir Richard began to find it annoying. He was pleased, naturally, that Saybrook was not giving his attention solely to Celia, but he would have been still more pleased had that gentleman not chosen Marguerite as an additional focus. He had studied her behavior since his talk with Celia the night of *Macbeth* and he had concluded that his first impression of her might very well have been a false one. He was fully prepared to say as much to her, and so it was annoying not to be able to do so. It was even more annoying when she appeared to have no interest in giving him any opportunity at all to speak with her.

Marguerite had become aware of his watchfulness, but she had interpreted it in her own way. Doubtless he was finding fault with her manner and her activities; he had done nothing save point out her shortcomings since first meeting her, so this did not come as any revelation to her. She had thought of thanking him for staying in Bath, for she had been quite sure that he had done it for their sake—or at least for Celia's sake. After having him study her as though she were under a lens, however, she had decided that she owed him no gratitude whatsoever. He *should* feel an obligation to look after young women under his protection, and so he deserved no special thanks for merely fulfilling his duties.

And so it was that as the time for the excursion to Mendassy grew near, Celia's difficult experiences seemed to have faded from public memory, and she and Marguerite were welcome everywhere. If anything, Celia's twin nightmares had made her more in demand than she might have been otherwise. And *everyone* wanted an invitation to Mendassy, to the fete planned in her honor. Lord Saybrook had known exactly the thing to do to restore her to public favor.

Marguerite watched with pleasure as her sister divided her attention among Lord Saybrook, Sir Richard, and Miles Randall. She seemed at ease with all three gentlemen and smiled upon them all without appearing to favor one over the other. Marguerite found herself hoping that young Randall would be the one Celia would settle upon, for the other two gentlemen seemed a danger to their peace of mind. She could not imagine that either Sir Richard or Lord Saybrook could make her sister happy—Sir Richard was too moody and Lord Saybrook too cynical.

The day before the gala affair was grey and rainy and a few of those eagerly awaiting the promised treat gathered gloomily in Lady Norwood's drawing room, attempting to convince themselves that the next day would be otherwise.

"For you know," said Miles cheerfully, "Saybrook always has his own way in everything, so we may rest assured that the weather will be cooperative tomorrow."

"You are too kind, Miles," drawled his friend. "I won't say that you are wrong, of course—but you *are,* nonetheless, kind to say it."

As the laughter which greeted this sally faded, Stephens announced Mr. Alexander Clive.

"Mr. Clive," said Marguerite in amazement, rising to take his hand and greet him in genuine pleasure. "How good it is to see you again!"

"I am pleased to see you and Miss Celia in such good spirits," returned the young clergyman. He looked somewhat abashed, for he had entered the room in the midst of their laughter, and he clearly was ill at ease in such a large and merry group. Sir Richard, noting the enthusiasm of Marguerite's greeting, wondered grimly what there was about such a shy young man that she would find so attractive.

Celia, too, held out her hand, but her expression was worried. "Is it Mrs. Ruscombe?" she asked quietly. "Has something happened?"

"No," he assured her quickly. "Mrs. Ruscombe remains just as she has been." Then, searching for words, he added, "I had business in the area, and I wished to be sure that you were both happy and well—and to see if I could be of any service to you."

"How kind of you," said Marguerite warmly, wondering what business could have brought him so far from home. "Mr. Clive became rector after our father's death," she said aloud, turning to introduce him to the others, "and he was very generous in helping us."

Before she could complete the introductions, Lady Norwood interrupted. "So *you* are the one! Young man, have you found a locket at the rectory? Have you come to deliver it?" she demanded sharply.

Mr. Clive turned to her, startled both by her question and her tone. "A locket?" he inquired mildly. Then his brow cleared. "Oh, the locket Miss Standish wrote about! No, I'm afraid not," he responded. "And I have searched very carefully."

Marguerite, whose cheeks had flamed at the mention of the locket, said calmly, "I'm certain that you did, Mr. Clive, and we are very grateful for your help."

Lady Norwood sank back on her sofa, her energy apparently depleted by this exertion.

Conversation became general, and the topic again was the trip to Mendassy.

"Perhaps, Mr. Clive, you might be able to join us tomorrow?" said Lord Saybrook with unwonted politeness.

"You are very kind, sir," returned the young clergyman, absently polishing his spectacles, "but I am afraid that I must be leaving for home tomorrow."

"Oh, do stay, Mr. Clive," urged Celia, leaning toward him, her eyes pleading. "You have had no opportunity to tell us about Northaven. Please stay so that we may hear all about everything that has happened since we left."

Mr. Clive paused in his polishing and looked at her closely. "If it would please you, Miss Celia," he began.

"Oh, it would, Mr. Clive, it would!" she exclaimed.

"Another conquest, Miles," murmured Saybrook in a voice too low to be heard by Mr. Clive. "You must watch yourself. The competition grows stiffer."

Sir Richard, who had overheard him, studied Celia's unusual animation. It might be that Lord Saybrook was quite correct in his joking comment.

Young Mr. Clive, clearly uncomfortable in his exalted company, soon excused himself, promising to join the group at the river the next morning. After his departure the conversation again focused on their anxieties about the weather, and continued in that vein until Lady Norwood could bear it no longer and announced that she and her guests needed their rest. She was not, of course, particularly concerned about her guests, but she had no intention of retiring to her chamber and leaving them to hold court in the drawing room. Reluctantly, the callers took themselves away, all of them predicting fair weather for the morrow.

Fortunately for the peace of mind of a good many young people in Bath, the day of the promised excursion dawned sunny and clear. At an early point in the day, the eager guests boarded the flower-bedecked barges that Lord Saybrook had waiting, and they began their leisurely journey down the Avon. The last barge carried the musicians, who serenaded them for the entire trip, their lilting melodies lifting the hearts of any who had not yet entered into the spirit of the day.

Marguerite sat on a cushioned bench, lost in the misty greenness of the passing scene and listening to the music, which shifted suddenly from the bright notes of a country dance to the haunting strains of a gypsy love song. Marguerite's eyes darkened as she trailed a reed in the water and watched its gentle wake.

"Don't tell me, dear lady, that you are mourning for a lost love," said Lord Saybrook softly, seating himself close beside her.

Marguerite looked up abruptly and smiled. "Whatever would make you say that, sir?"

"Your very sad expression, Miss Standish. Your eyes look as though you are remembering a time that is lost forever, never to come again."

"You are very perceptive, Lord Saybrook," she complimented him. "I was remembering such a time—but not a time spent with a lover."

"A thousand pities, then, dear lady," he returned, taking her hand. "You were made for tender memories."

Reclaiming her hand with a smile and plucking a wild rose from the wreath of flowers he had crowned her with earlier, she tucked it into the band of his hat. "And you, sir," she replied lightly, "were made for light flirtations."

"That might have been true of me a month ago, Miss Standish—or even a week ago—but not now. No longer do I dally." Here he took her hand again. "Now I say with all seriousness that I did not know what I was lacking until I knew you. Now when I walk into a crowded room, it is your face that I search for. When I hear a woman speak, I measure her voice by the melody of yours."

Marguerite stared at him in surprise, for his tone had the ring of truth, and he no longer wore his quizzical expression or spoke in a teasing voice.

"You are wondering about me," he said, smiling. "It is true that I have changed—and it is true that you have become my standard for what a woman should be."

"What do you mean, Lord Saybrook?" she managed to stammer. "You have known me only for a very short time. How could you believe that you know so much about me?"

"I have made it my business to know your every move, to watch your every expression. I know that you would do anything for your young sister, and I would do anything to command such a loyal love as yours."

Marguerite leaned toward him, for the moment lost to everything else about them save his unexpectedly tender expression, not at all what she would have connected with the careless lord. It made him seem more vulnerable than a boy. She touched his cheek softly, then sat back on her bench, recalled to her surroundings by a homely halloo from shore as they approached the docks at Mendassy. As she rose from her place for a better view, she reminded herself that Saybrook's pretty speech was very likely the product of a fleeting affection. She had watched Saybrook and recognized that he was one who must always be in love—or at least have an object for his affections.

Sir Richard, riding on the barge behind them, had witnessed this byplay and had longed to be able to put a stop to it as quickly as possible. Unfortunately, trapped as he was, all that he could do was to wish that he could remove Marguerite swiftly to a safer atmosphere and that he could send Saybrook to Jericho. He was not too pleased that Celia was seated between Miles Randall and the young clergyman, but that was far preferable to the company Marguerite was keeping. Having two young houseguests was proving more of a responsibility than he had planned.

He glanced at his stepmother, who appeared unconcerned by the activities of those young ladies. She was absorbed by an aging but attentive beau, who had just composed a sonnet about her eyebrows. Lady Norwood—as he had already guessed—would be of no help as a chaperone. He would have to take care of matters himself.

Marguerite had turned away from Lord Saybrook to the spectacle that lay before her. Mendassy was everything she had thought it would be. Lord Saybrook was justly proud of his home. It was a classical scholar's dream. The house itself, a graceful rise of cream stone, overlooked the Avon, its terraced gardens gently descending to the river. In the distance an artificial lake was visible, a small Grecian temple standing on its one green island.

The musicians were soon established on an upper terrace, and their melodies drifted down to the revelers. Saybrook's guests were welcomed into the house and wandered about to admire the great marble hall with its colonnaded courtyard and graceful statues of gods and goddesses, the long gallery with its wealth of portraits and paintings by artists as diverse as Reynolds and Reubens, the sun-filled sculpture gallery that overlooked a topiary garden.

They dined *al fresco* in the charming gardens, wandering at will over the carefully manicured grounds. There were games for the younger guests, and ample time for rest and conversation for the older ones before the opening of an informal ball. Sir Richard found himself far busier than he wished to be, for his two young charges moved in opposite directions, Marguerite and Saybrook drifting toward the gardens, while Celia and her two admirers strolled along the riverbank.

To Sir Richard's irritation, Saybrook opened the ball with Marguerite and led Celia out for the second dance. Since it was his understanding that Saybrook was vindicating Celia, he felt that she should have been the one to open the ball. Saybrook was showing more attention to Marguerite than was good for her reputation—more, he feared, than might be good for her affections, for Saybrook was a consummate flirt. He noted, too, that Marguerite appeared to be enjoying herself far too much. Intent upon reminding her of the manner of man Saybrook was, he asked her to walk with him in the privacy of a walled garden, fresh with spring flowers.

"I am aware that you are new to our ways, Miss Standish," he began, sounding somewhat pompous even to himself. "And so I am taking the liberty of warning you against allowing the too intimate attentions of Lord Saybrook."

"Are you referring to the gentleman who has been kind enough to hold this entertainment so that Celia and I may be accepted in Bath?" she inquired sharply.

Being called to book in such a manner was distasteful to Sir Richard, but he accepted his rebuke as mildly as possible, reminding her that gratitude can sometimes make one more susceptible.

"Do you mean that I might find myself compromised, Sir Richard?" she asked in amusement.

He nodded briefly, deploring her directness.

"You need not worry on my account, sir." She paused for a moment, as though deep in thought. "However, should Saybrook decide to offer for me, I would be forced to consider it, you know. After all, he is a charming man—and I do enjoy the way he lives."

Sir Richard took her arm ungently and turned her towards him. "Why must you always be so perverse?" he demanded, his face even darker than usual. "I am aware, Miss Standish, that you go out of your way to bait me. Why do you insist upon trying to annoy me?"

Curiously pleased by this show of emotion, she smiled beatifically. "It must be that your gentlemanly behavior calls out the best in me, Sir Richard."

He glared at her for a moment and then, taking both of them by surprise, he pulled her into his arms and kissed her soundly. More surprising to both of them was the pleasure that it offered. Marguerite felt as though the warmth of the summer sun were melting her very bones.

She was a little unsteady when she emerged from his embrace, but she regained her composure first, inquiring demurely, "Is that how you feared Lord Saybrook would treat me, sir? It is kind of you to demonstrate so that I would not be in any doubt if he went beyond the line in his behavior."

She did not wait for a response, but left him standing there, certain that he was quite as angry and shaken as she. Irritated by the truth of her observation, he longed to shake her until her teeth rattled, and promised himself that he would not allow her to annoy him in such a manner in the future. Then, as he grew calmer, he was forced to admit to himself that his behavior had scarcely been that of a gentleman. More than that, he had begun to like her altogether too much, especially since he had come to accept Celia's evaluation of her. And he knew that Marguerite delighted in placing him in the most unfavorable light possible. Unfortunately, he reflected ruefully, that had not been too difficult to accomplish.

That evening the sisters were quiet on the carriage ride home. Lady Norwood had her own carriage, and Sir Richard rode alongside, so there was little reason for them to guard their tongues.

"Are you very tired, Celia dear?" inquired Marguerite at last, turning her gaze from the full moon shining across the meadows to her sister.

Celia shook her head, her hair gleaming as silvery as the moonlight. It was no wonder that Sir Richard looked at her so often, Marguerite mused. How could anyone resist such a vision? She sighed and shook herself.

"Do you think that Mr. Clive had a good time?" she asked absently, trying to elicit some sort of response from Celia.

"I don't think so," she responded in a low voice. "I think that he must be very depressed, Marguerite."

"Why should he be depressed? Why would he not enjoy an outing such as this?"

"It isn't that, Marguerite. Oh, I feel so very sorry for him, and there was really nothing I could say to him that would help matters!" she exclaimed.

Marguerite stared at her. "What were you trying to help, Celia? What is wrong with Mr. Clive?"

"His fiancée cried off—and just before the wedding! The poor man must be demoralized!"

"He didn't appear so," said Marguerite a little dryly, remembering his stroll with Celia along the banks of the Avon and his dance with her later in the evening.

"Of course he doesn't allow himself to appear so!" returned Celia, with what could almost be called a snap.

Marguerite looked at her sister in astonishment. Celia never spoke sharply. It was astounding what life with Sir Richard had done for her.

"He doesn't share his troubles with the world," continued Celia defensively.

"He appears to have shared them with you," said Marguerite, more dryly still.

"Only because I asked him," replied Celia. "Otherwise, he would have simply answered my questions about Northaven and gone quietly home again tomorrow."

They were silent for a few moments, then Celia added with a sigh, "It was so delightful to hear all about Northaven, Marguerite—you've no idea how I've missed it and longed to know what was happening. And it was so kind of him to call and tell me all about things there."

"Yes, it certainly was," agreed Marguerite absently, troubled by her sister's revelation. Not only did Celia have a new suitor, but she also was homesick for Northaven. Who would have thought that she would truly miss the place? Misgivings assailed her once again. Had she been wrong to bring Celia to London and Bath? Then she remembered Vincent Beezley and sat a little straighter. There had been no other choice.

"Marguerite?" Celia's voice trembled a little, and Marguerite reached out and took her outstretched hand. "He goes home tomorrow." And she buried her face on her sister's shoulder and wept.

Marguerite, secretly relieved that the young rector would soon be far away, stroked her sister's hair and murmured soothingly, deliberately conjuring up an image of Vincent Beezley. Again she told herself that there had been no other choice. Once a few days had passed, Celia would be happy again. Mr. Clive had merely brought a fresh attack of homesickness for a home that no longer existed. Their future was here.

Fifteen

After Mendassy, it seemed clear to Marguerite that any social problems that she and Celia had had were well behind them. They were in demand at every breakfast and ball, for, as Lord Saybrook had foreseen, being acknowledged by him had assured their favorable reception by the others. He might have a reputation as a rake, but he was also an acknowledged leader in that part of the world and a marital prize of great consequence. Many a mother had hoped that her daughter would be the one to lead him to the altar.

Celia was very quiet for a few days following the excursion, but she gradually became more animated. Marguerite was pleased to see that she seemed to be developing a partiality for Miles Randall, who remained studiously attentive, calling in the Crescent daily, sending flowers, bringing Nipper packets of particularly succulent seeds. Also, to her intense relief, there had been no more unpleasant incidents involving Celia, and no more warning notes. She still carried the last one on her person, afraid that it, too, would disappear from her room, but she had begun to feel that there was really no need for such precautions. Even her note to the intruder was still in place.

Since she still felt positive that Tolliver was the culprit, she took every opportunity to inspect the maid's handwriting. So far, however, she had found only a brief recipe for a cucumber cream for Lady Norwood's complexion. Marguerite could not be certain of the handwriting, for that on the warning notes had been, she was sure, disguised. Nonetheless, there were enough similarities to fuel her suspicions.

Now that Tolliver had seen that they were no threat to her or her mistress, it seemed reasonable that she would feel no need to write any more of the notes. The maid appeared to be reconciled to their presence in the household, and, although she made no friendly overtures, she no longer directed unpleasant remarks or darkling glances toward them. All in all, Marguerite grew hopeful that life had now truly changed for them, and her goal of settling Celia happily and safely appeared to be well within her reach.

She was certain that Miles Randall would offer for Celia soon, and she found herself wondering what Sir Richard would think of that. He was undoubtedly fond of Celia, but he showed no jealousy of Miles, chatting with the couple amiably whenever he encountered them, watching them dance with obvious pleasure. If Marguerite thought now and then that it would be pleasant to talk with him more often—or even to argue with him a little—she did not admit this to herself. Whenever the memory of the kiss in the walled garden at Mendassy troubled her, she dismissed it as quickly as possible. It had meant nothing to him—and certainly less than that to her. Lord Saybrook remained attentive to her, too, although he had not again declared himself. From time to time she wondered idly if he would.

Finally, too, she acknowledged to herself that she had done Lady Norwood an injustice by keeping her locket from her, and she decided that she must return it. She had been reluctant to do so, partially because she had been afraid that the Norwoods would look upon it as an act of theft, and she and Celia had already had too much trouble with matters such as that. Nevertheless, after Mr. Clives' visit, she had at last decided that she must be forthright— or at least reasonably so.

She wanted to show Celia the locket first in privacy

and, accordingly, called her into her chamber one evening before going down to dinner.

"Celia, here is the locket I found in Mama's trunk," she said, holding out her hand with the locket lying on her palm.

"Is this what Mr. Clive was looking for? Where did you find it, Marguerite?" her sister exclaimed, lifting it carefully and examining the scrollwork on its surface.

"I knew where it was all of the time, Celia," she confessed. "I just didn't wish to give it to Lady Norwood."

Celia stared at her. "Why not, Marguerite?" she asked, puzzled. "Don't you think it belongs to her?"

"Yes, of course I do—but I didn't like what was happening when we first arrived. I thought that I would just wait a day or two to give it to her—but then we had the trouble of the bracelet and the lace, and I didn't feel that I dared show it then. I was afraid that they would accuse me of theft."

Celia nodded, her expression unusually grim. "No. I hadn't thought about it like that, but you were right to be afraid, Marguerite. You made a wise decision."

"That isn't what I'm going to tell Lady Norwood, though," Marguerite warned her. "I'm merely going to say that I found it in the lining of my sewing basket."

Celia nodded again. "That's a good idea."

Marguerite opened the locket. "Here is the other reason that I hated to give it up."

Celia looked down and gasped. "Why, she looks just like Mama!" she exclaimed softly. "I can't believe it!"

"And just like you," added Marguerite. "We never had a miniature of Mama, and it almost felt as though I were giving away a picture of her to a stranger."

Celia nodded, still staring at the miniatures. "And he is a very striking man, isn't he? They must have been very handsome together."

She looked at it for a moment longer, then added, "I

know that Mama said that she was related to Lady Norwood, but I hadn't dreamed that she would look so much like Lady Norwood's mother."

The two girls studied the face in the miniature, so like that of their mother. Finally, Marguerite said slowly, "I have been wondering just how closely Mama might have been related to her ever since I saw this, Celia. It had occurred to me that they might have had the same father."

Celia's eyebrows drew together as she thought this over. "Had the same father? Do you mean that Mama might have been born out of wedlock, Marguerite?"

Marguerite nodded. "That is what I thought when I first saw this locket. That's why I didn't want to tell you about it, Celia. I was afraid that it would upset you."

"Poor Mama," said Celia softly. "Do you think that she knew it?"

"How could she have seen the Marquise de Valencia and not have thought it? The likeness between them is too striking."

"But the Marquise must have seen the likeness, too, Marguerite. Why would she have tolerated it? She could have sent Mama away, couldn't she?"

"She could have done so, of course. But our grandmother had come with her as her companion when she married. Very likely they were good friends—and, at any rate, Mama would not have looked so much like her until she was grown, and she was no more than eighteen when she left France forever."

Celia stared at the miniatures once more, then closed the locket resolutely and handed it back to her sister. "I can see why you had trouble parting with it, Marguerite. If I looked at it for one more minute, I would feel the same way. I think that we had best go down to dinner."

Marguerite smiled and hugged her. "We will have a miniature painted of you, Celia. I should imagine that your husband will have your portrait painted as soon as you are married—and I will at least have a miniature of my own. It will be like having a picture of both you and Mama."

"I don't know why you are speaking of my husband, Marguerite," she said, blushing. "No one has offered for me as yet."

"Ah, but that will change very soon, my dear. I have been watching Mr. Randall."

Celia tried to smile as she entered the drawing room, looking grateful that they were joining the others so that she was spared any further conversation. Marguerite, faced now with the obligation of presenting the locket, took her courage in her hands and approached her hostess.

"Lady Norwood, I have a surprise for you," she said, managing a creditable sprightliness of tone. Opening her hand, she disclosed the locket.

"You found it!" exclaimed Lady Norwood.

"Yes," Marguerite replied, coloring a little as she spoke. "I opened my sewing basket and I felt a lump in the lining when I moved the pin cushion. The locket had slipped down in the padding of the lining."

"How fortunate that you had some sewing to do," said Philippe, coming over to look down at the locket.

He gazed down at the miniatures for a moment or two, then took the open locket from his mother and went over to the pier glass, holding it up beside his face and studying the reflections in the mirror. "I think there is a certain likeness there, don't you?"

Sir Richard, who had come to stand beside him, stared down at the locket for a moment and then looked up sharply at Celia. Marguerite, watching him carefully, waited for him to speak. Instead of saying anything, however, he walked away from Philippe and stood looking out the window across the Crescent Fields.

"I think there is a decided resemblance, dear boy," said his mother. "Come here and let me see the locket again before you fasten it about my neck."

Obediently, Philippe brought it over to her, and they sat side by side for a moment, pointing out the similarities they saw between Philippe and the Marquis. Marguerite, for her part, could trace no likeness at all, and she was astounded that there had been no comment about the marked resemblance between the Marquise and Celia. For a moment she almost wondered whether or not the resemblance was a real one, or whether she had just imagined it. Since Celia had noticed it immediately, however, she felt that she had not been mistaken. It must surely be that Lady Norwood and Philippe so much longed for a resemblance to his grandfather that they perceived a likeness where there was none, and had no thought of making any other comparisons.

"Well, Marguerite, you have done me a great kindness by giving me this locket. I am very grateful," said Lady Norwood as Philippe fastened it about her neck. "I will keep it close to me always. Aside from her jewels, I have nothing personal that belonged to my dear mother, and of course this is the only likeness I have of my father as well. And it is the first time that Philippe has seen either of them."

Marguerite, a little ashamed that she had not relinquished it earlier, murmured that she had been glad to do it, and hoped that her expression would not give her away. She glanced toward Sir Richard, and saw that he was watching her with a sardonic expression. She felt the warmth flooding her cheeks and was thoroughly annoyed with him. Her guilt for her deception about the locket weighed heavily upon her, and she felt as though he could see right through her and knew about every detail of her subterfuge.

All in all, she was most grateful when the evening was finally over. They had listened to countless tales of life in France and the beauty of the Marquise and the cleverness and courage of the Marquis, and they had heard of Philppe's plans to establish himself on de Valencia lands as soon as the war was over. There was such a steady diet of old times that she found it difficult to sustain an expression of intelligent interest in the stories. She did not wish to insult her hostess, who was clearly enjoying herself, but it grew more and more difficult to pay attention.

When the gentlemen joined them for coffee in the drawing room after dinner, Sir Richard joined her at the window and murmured, "A most remarkable likeness, did you not think so, Miss Standish?"

"Philippe does look a great deal like his grandfather," she said cautiously, willing to perjure herself a second time.

"That is not what I mean, Miss Standish, as you well know," he said in a low voice. "I am astounded that you have not mentioned it yourself. You surely perceive it."

Marguerite attempted to look appropriately uninformed and unaware, but he dismissed her with a wave of the hand. "I have no patience with pretense, Miss Standish. You should know that by now."

"If you mean by that that you frequently dispense with good manners, Sir Richard, I would be compelled to agree with you," she said frigidly, attempting to set him in his place and failing entirely.

"Bravo, Miss Standish! A home shot!" he applauded her. "I suppose that I am scarcely a paragon of social virtues," he said.

"Scarcely!" she sniffed in agreement. "You have no social virtues at all that I can detect, sir," she informed him.

He bowed, accepting her insult as a tribute. "You honor me, madam," he assured her.

There are few things more aggravating than those who will not grow angry when they should. It is disturbing to those about them who react in a more predictable fashion.

"And you know, Sir Richard, that there was nothing farther from my mind than doing so," she returned firmly.

He again bowed, and then smiled at her obvious irritation. "I must confess, ma'am, that I suspected as much."

"Then you might have had the good breeding not to bait me," she snapped.

"Perhaps," he returned smoothly, "but I knew that I would disappoint you if I accidentally revealed some trace of good behavior."

Before she could reply, he continued, looking down at her thoughtfully. "Then, too, I would have denied myself the pleasure of seeing you become thoroughly incensed, Miss Standish. It is charming to watch the rush of color into your cheek as you first grow angry, then to see your lips tighten and your eyes grow wider and brighter as you try to conceal any evidence of your emotion." He stopped again and smiled disarmingly. "It is a most impossible task, you do realize. There is no hope of your concealing your emotions from onlookers, Miss Standish. You are quite transparent."

"I feel that I must say good night, sir," she said shortly, turning to beckon to Celia and to say her good night to her host and hostess.

As she swept from the room with Celia in her wake, Sir Richard watched her speculatively, still wondering about the locket. Turning back to Lady Norwood and Philippe, he bowed shortly.

"I must thank you for your hospitality, ma'am," he said impassively.

"You know very well that it is your own hospitality," Lady Norwood snapped. "In this as in everything else we must rely upon your charity. I suppose that if you decided to cast me out into the streets, I should simply starve, having no resources of my own."

"Not at all, ma'am," he returned smoothly. "I would not, of course, so turn my back on my responsibilities as to do what you have just described. If I did, however, I have every confidence that you would not starve—say what you will, you are a most resourceful woman." And here his eyes wandered to the locket at her throat.

She flushed and covered it with her hand. "I suppose that you begrudge me even this little bit of my past, Richard. It must gall you to think that Philippe and I are of a nobler family than your own."

"I begrudge you nothing, ma'am, that is your own." Bowing once again, he left the drawing room and saw himself out the front door leading onto the Crescent.

Sixteen

The next morning Marguerite jerked upright in bed as a series of screams ripped through the predawn silence of the household. Pulling on her dressing gown, she joined Celia, Lady Norwood, Philippe, and an assortment of servants on the stairs. Stephens appeared at the base of the steps, his nightcap askew and his expression grim.

"It's Tolliver, my lady. Mary found her dead in the kitchen."

Celia and Marguerite reached out to support Lady Norwood, who suddenly looked as though she might pitch forward down the steps. She sat down abruptly, staring at the butler. "Tolliver?" she said blankly. "Tolliver can't be dead. Of course she is not. Send for a surgeon, Stephens," she said to the butler.

Stephens nodded and sent one of the footmen hurrying out into the early morning streets.

"Come, Lady Norwood," said Celia soothingly, putting her arm around that lady's shoulders. "Let me take you back to your room. I think that you should lie down."

Lady Norwood allowed herself to be led up the stairs like a child, and Marguerite, certain that Celia had matters there in hand for the moment, followed Philippe and Stephens and the cook to the kitchen. The kitchenmaid who had found her was no longer in hysterics, but had subsided into a low, steady sobbing as she rocked back and forward, her arms crossed over her breast. Marguerite went back to the stairs where the two other maids were still waiting, and told them to come and take her up to the room they shared in the garret.

Tolliver lay crumpled on the brick floor in front of the stone fireplace, one arm outstretched. The fire had not yet been started; that had been Mary's job. Marguerite caught a glimpse of white at the edge of Tolliver's dark gown and knelt down to examine it. One look told her that it was the note that she had left in her lap desk.

"Did you find something?" asked Philippe curiously.

"No, not really," she responded, slipping the bit of paper into the sleeve of her nightgown. She smoothed Tolliver's skirt, as though that was what she had intended to do. "I wonder what could have brought her downstairs at such an hour," she said, thinking to herself that Tolliver had probably been hoping for a fire in which to burn the note she had taken from the lap desk.

"She probably came down to fix herself a cup of tea," observed Philippe without emotion. "She has always had trouble sleeping at night—she never seems to need as much rest as most people."

"Do you think it was apoplexy?" asked Marguerite, staring down at her and trying not to think that there would be no more trouble with warning notes. Even though she had not liked Tolliver, it seemed wrong to feel any gladness because of another's death.

Philippe shrugged. "Who could say?" he responded. "I doubt that the surgeon will know either. They're useless fellows, all of them, who take your money and tell you their best guesses about things. There was really no reason to send for him."

"I believe that your mother will need him," said Marguerite, amazed that he had not taken Lady Norwood's state into account. "And you will need to make a report about the death at any rate."

Philippe shrugged again, as though none of this mattered very much to him, and turned to start back up the stairs.

A pretty sad state of affairs, reflected Marguerite. Tolliver had been with this family for more than twenty-one years, and Philippe acted as though her death were of no more account than the inconvenient action of a stranger.

Marguerite followed him to his mother's room, where the kindhearted Celia sat beside Lady Norwood's bed, alternately bathing her forehead and administering smelling salts as she murmured to her comfortingly.

"Whatever will I do without Tolliver?" she cried in a plaintive voice, clutching Celia's wrist. "She has always looked after me. Who will take care of me now?"

"Why, we will, of course," replied Celia calmly, and Marguerite groaned inwardly. Once again Celia was going to sacrifice herself for someone's else's convenience and comfort, and it sounded as though she had included Marguerite into the bargain.

Lady Norwood stopped her frenzied crying for a moment, and stared up at her. Just then the surgeon appeared in the doorway, however, and Lady Norwood returned to her crying and moaning. He administered the sedative promptly and smoothly, and gradually her stormy sobbing faded into a more peaceful, distant crying. Celia sat with her until the crying had stopped and Lady Norwood finally slept. Having been assured by the surgeon that she would now sleep for several hours, Celia installed one of the housemaids in her place and stole gratefully downstairs for a cup of tea.

She joined Marguerite in the dining room, where breakfast waited on the sideboard. The household was running smoothly, quite as though Tolliver's death had been no more than a ripple in the quiet pond of domestic life.

"Philippe has already eaten and gone out riding," said Marguerite dryly. "No doubt he was overcome by grief and needed to be alone for a while."

Celia looked at her reprovingly. "Not everyone shows their emotions openly, Marguerite. I am sure that he felt some attachment for Tolliver. After all, he has known her all of his life."

Knowing that it would be useless to argue with her sister, Marguerite murmured something that could be interpreted as agreement—although it was not—and insisted that Celia take more than tea for her breakfast. She resisted at first, but finally succumbed when Marguerite pointed out that she would need her strength if she were to be of service to Lady Norwood.

"I left Betsy watching over her," Celia said, toying with a piece of toast. "The surgeon said that Lady Norwood will sleep at least until late afternoon. Then we are to feed her some nourishing broth and administer another dose of the medicine. I am sure that it will do her good to rest for such a long time. Perhaps when she awakens, she will feel more prepared to deal with Tolliver's death. After all, with our mother gone, she was Lady Norwood's last link with her home and childhood. She must be feeling very lonely."

Marguerite reflected guiltily that she had not thought of that, and felt a renewed respect for her younger sister. Celia never failed to be able to view a problem from someone else's perspective and was always astonished when others were surprised by her comments. For the thousandth time she reminded herself that Celia's clarity of vision was because of a lack of selfishness. Putting yourself into the scene only kept you from seeing clearly.

"I am sure that you are right, Celia," she said, crumbling her own toast into crumbs and feeling suddenly desolate. "I can imagine how lonely I would feel if I were suddenly completely alone—and no longer had you." She had no need to exaggerate. She thought of Celia marrying someone who would take her away. Sir Richard would separate them psychologically; Mr. Clive, physically. Either one would be unbearable.

Celia smiled and patted her hand encouragingly, for once playing the role of counselor and comforter. "But you will always have me, Marguerite. Whether we set up housekeeping together or whether one of us finds a husband, we will always be together."

"What a charming scene of sisterly devotion," said Philippe, settling himself in an elegant pose at the head of the table. "I do think that I could count myself the most fortunate of men if I were to marry one of you lovely ladies and have you both living here with me."

"And is Bath where you plan to settle, Mr. Norwood?" inquired Marguerite, eager to place the conversation on a less personal plane. She had noticed that recently he had been much more attentive to Celia, and the mere thought of her sister married to him was unsettling. He was a very handsome, eligible man, and he could be charming company whenever he chose to be. But then, of course, he was quite as selfish as his mother, so Celia would again be taken advantage of.

A crease appeared on his flawless brow as he answered her question. "Only temporarily, Miss Standish," he replied coolly. "I will, of course, be journeying to France as soon as it is possible to straighten out my affairs there."

"Of course," Marguerite murmured. "I am certain that you are eager for that day to come."

"How could I not be?" Philippe returned, his face growing darker. "I am hemmed in at every point now, forced to live on the charity of my brother and to abide by his rules as though I were no more than a child in the nursery! It is more than flesh and bone can bear!"

Marguerite pondered that remark for a moment. So Sir Richard did provide his support—and undoubtedly that of Lady Norwood, as well. She suddenly remembered that lady's barbed comment about her husband's desire to cut his son out of his will. He had died unexpectedly, however, with no opportunity to do so. A curious coincidence, that.

Realizing the implications of her thoughts, Marguerite rose abruptly and walked to the window, so absorbed that she was unconscious of the fact that Philippe and Celia were staring after her. Perhaps Lady Norwood had been right about her reading material. Although she seldom read gothics, she must surely have been too much influenced by the few that she had read, or she would not be having thoughts like these. She shook her head firmly. She might not be overly fond of Sir Richard—he was too arrogant and too careless of her feelings for that to be possible—but she could not picture him murdering his own father.

"I am certain that it must be difficult," she replied at last, turning back to Philippe and attempting to soothe his ruffled pride. "At least Sir Richard is not usually with you. I understand that he lives most of the year at Greenwood Park."

Philippe gave a brief, sharp laugh. "Why should he not?" he demanded petulantly. "Perhaps I would do so, too, if Greenwood Park had come to me as our father intended it should! If I were surrounded by interesting people and my books, as well as one of the finest stables in the country, I might well be happy!"

Marguerite reflected that she had never seen Philippe with a book in his hand, and he was an indifferent horseman.

"I know that he loves his books and his horses, Philippe, but who are the interesting people?" she inquired, well aware that Philippe had hoped that she would ask about why Sir Richard had inherited the estate when their father had intended it for Philippe. She was too curious to do anything other than ask her own question first.

Irritated by her lack of interest, Philippe lifted one shoulder pettishly. "Just the usual rabble, looking for a country holiday away from London, and too cheap to take lodgings on their own—actors, a writer or two, some of the more troublesome members of the House of Lords."

Marguerite's eyes sparkled. Perhaps living at Greenwood Park would not mean that she must give up all hope of amusement and conversation with the outside world. If Celia were to marry Sir Richard, she would be perfectly happy in the rural setting of Greenwood Park, and, if Philippe were correct, there might even be some prospect of happiness there for Marguerite. It would, of course, be a trial to be a member of the same household as Sir Richard, but she could get along nicely if there were a variety of entertaining guests.

She tried to make her tone more sympathetic than she felt. "And do you visit often, Mr. Norwood?" she asked. "It must be difficult to spend time at a place that you once thought would be your own."

He seized upon that immediately. "I knew that you would understand, Miss Standish!" he exclaimed, his expression lightening. "I seldom go to Greenwood for that very reason. And Richard feels not even the slightest remorse for taking it from me! Why, whenever I pointed out last Christmas that the estate should have been mine and he should have been visiting *me* there for the holidays, he merely stared at me through that damned glass of his as though I were some kind of bug he were studying."

Marguerite murmured something vaguely sympathetic, and Philippe continued, his eyes growing more fiery. "I told him that he had no right to be standing there in the library with that portrait of our father looking down on us. He had the unmitigated gall to lecture me about my insignificant gambling debts when he did not blink at spending a small fortune on improvements for the home farm and for the cottages of some of the tenants. I told him that *I* should not have spent the money in such a wasteful manner!"

"And what did he reply to that?" she inquired mildly, a little taken aback by such open selfishness.

"He merely laughed and said that I was telling him nothing that he did not already know. And then he said, 'My father knew that, too, Philippe. He would never have allowed you to control the estate.' "

"You must have been very distressed by that," Marguerite said encouragingly, when he did not immediately continue.

"I ripped off my glove and threw it in his face," replied Philippe, his voice ripe with satisfaction. "He did not accept the challenge, of course, for he knows that I am reckoned excellent with either pistol or sword."

"What did he say?"

Philippe's smile faded. "He laughed again, and told me to save such fustian for plays at school, as though I were a mere schoolboy!"

"That must have been frustrating," she responded sympathetically, thinking that it must have been even more difficult for Sir Richard, confronted with such melodramatic posturing.

"Again you understand!" he exclaimed, taking her hand impulsively. "Please allow me to take you and your sister for a drive, Miss Standish. This has been very trying for you both, and some fresh air is the very thing you need to revive you."

Looking at Celia's pale face, Marguerite accepted gratefully. She could bear more of Philippe's stories for the sake of getting her sister out into the country. Eager to leave the gloom of the house behind them for a little while, the girls hurried upstairs to change for the drive while he ordered the carriage.

The day was lovely and, to Marguerite's relief, Philippe appeared to feel no need to unburden himself further. She was free to relax and enjoy the quiet greenness of the countryside. She was feeling almost restored to her usual composure as they crested one of the seven hills of Bath and looked down on the Avon winding peacefully below them. Nearby was a tiny inn and Philippe suggested that they stop for some refreshment.

Gratefully they accepted his offer and seated themselves on a bench at the front of the inn so that they could enjoy the charming view, and Philippe went inside to find the innkeeper. A few minutes later he appeared, bearing two glasses of lemonade and a cup of ale for himself.

"And here we are, ladies," he announced cheerfully. "I believe that you will find this to your taste."

As Marguerite lifted her glass, a voice said gently, "I don't believe that I would drink any of that lemonade, Miss Standish."

All of them looked up, startled. Sir Richard was leaning against the balustrade of the tiny porch. Behind him was the horse he had arrived on.

"And why should I not, Sir Richard?" she inquired, looking longingly at the cool glass she had set down after his warning. Celia, too, had taken her hand from her glass.

"I think that you would not feel well after drinking it," he replied dryly, looking at Philippe, whose eyes were blazing.

"And what do you mean by that, Richard?" he demanded. "Am I not to drink my ale?"

"Oh, I think your ale would be quite safe," responded Sir Richard. "It is the lemonade that I mistrust."

Marguerite and Celia stared at him, still not certain of his meaning, but Philippe was on his feet, his hands clenched. "You have pressed me too far this time, Richard! You have always hated me and looked for ways to discredit me, but *this!* This is beyond anything!"

"Very impressive, Philippe," returned Sir Richard, nodding appreciatively at his performance. "You could earn my profound apologies in a moment by merely drinking the lemonade yourself."

With a single motion Philippe dashed the drinks from

the table, spilling them across the grass beside the porch, then snatched the bridle of Sir Richard's horse and threw himself into the saddle. The girls sat mesmerized as he galloped away down the road to Bath in a cloud of dust.

Sir Richard eased himself onto the bench beside them. "You don't really think that there was anything wrong with the lemonade, do you, Sir Richard?" asked Celia a little weakly.

Sir Richard patted her hand reassuringly. "I think it very likely, Celia. But I don't think that you have anything more to fear from Philippe."

"But why should we have had anything to fear from him in the first place?" demanded Marguerite suddenly. To her amazement she found herself unfolding the warning note that she always carried with her. "With Tolliver gone, should we not have been freed from any future problem?" She handed Sir Richard the note. He read it carefully, eyebrows lifted.

"And I found this next to Tolliver's body," she said, giving him the one that she had hidden in her lap desk. "She took it from among my things, just as she did with the original warning that was mailed to us in Northaven."

"So it was Tolliver," he murmured, extricating a note of his own from his pocketbook and setting it on the table beside the one Marguerite had handed him. "I thought that it had to be."

Marguerite stared at him and then at the papers before them. "Do you mean that you have received warnings as well?"

"I received that one—the last one—when I was twenty-three. My father and I had become estranged—thanks to the efforts of the delightful Marguerite de Valencia."

Marguerite smoothed out his note and read it. It was in the same handwriting that her own two had been written in. This note warned Sir Richard to stay away from his father or he would place himself and his father in danger.

"I have kept this for years," he said, "hoping that some-day I would be able to identify the author. Now I know that it was Tolliver—and I think that she truly meant it as a warning, not a threat. I don't believe that she was the murderess."

"Murderess?" the sisters gasped in unison. "Who was murdered?"

"My father was," he returned grimly, staring at the de-lightful view before them without seeing it. "It was set about that he had had a heart attack, but I had received a letter from him just the day before, asking me to come and see him because he had something important to tell me. By the time I arrived, he was dead. And my dear stepmother, of course, said he had wanted to cut his ties with me—and she was prostrate with grief for weeks. But she was herself again in time for the Season and shop-ping," he added bitterly.

Marguerite had been sitting like one turned to stone. "Your father died of a heart attack?" she demanded. "And you think it was poison?"

He nodded, knowing what she was thinking. "His butler said that it happened very quickly. He grew flushed and hot, then he did not seem to know who or where he was, then he could not catch his breath and so collapsed—then died. All in a matter of a few minutes."

"That is the way the innkeeper's wife described our mother's death," whispered Celia, clutching Marguerite's hand.

"I know," replied Sir Richard grimly. "When I heard her account of it at The Rose and Thistle, I was more certain than before that I had been right—that my father had been murdered."

Marguerite straightened up angrily. "But you said noth-ing to us!" she blazed. "Why could you not have told us what you were thinking?"

"But, Marguerite, what was I to think? I did not know

you. I knew only that you were throwing yourselves upon the tender mercies of my stepmother—and that your own mother was her good friend. How could I be certain of how you fit into the matter at hand?"

"But how *do* we fit in?" mused Marguerite slowly. "Why should Philippe suddenly wish to kill us? And why would he have killed Tolliver—if indeed he did poison her, too?"

"I believe he must have been afraid that she was about to warn you again . . . and perhaps she was going to speak to you rather than merely writing to you."

"But why—" she began, then remembering the locket, she nodded. "I see. This has happened because of the locket. Is it because of the picture, do you think?" she asked, looking closely at Sir Richard.

He nodded. "I think perhaps there was an earlier murder as well. There was an elderly cousin who came to England with Marguerite de Valencia and Angelique D'Arcy. She died suddenly, a few weeks after their arrival in London."

Marguerite was silent as she considered this. "If the cousin was indeed killed, it must have been because she, too, was dangerous to someone. She was the only one who had come with them, the only one that they knew— or that knew them—in this new place."

"And, I believe, the only one who knew that Angelique was really Marguerite de Valencia," said Sir Richard calmly. "I am quite certain that they exchanged identities when they were trying to escape from France. Then, in case of anyone catching up with them before then, the real Marguerite would be able to slip away as Angelique D'Arcy."

"But why would they have switched names?" asked Celia.

"Probably to protect Marguerite, a member of the nobility, from any who might have tried to keep her from leaving the country or who might have tried to take her back to France from England, " replied Sir Richard.

"But what of Angelique?" she asked. "Was her life of no importance?"

"She was a servant," he returned frankly, "so it isn't likely that the Marquis would have considered her as important as his own daughter. Then, too, if they had been stopped and the real Marguerite allowed to go on, Angelique might have been able to prove her true identity and to say that she had been forced by Marguerite to assume her name. She might well have escaped the wrath of the revolutionaries with such a story."

"But why would Mama not have said anything to us during all of those years?" mused Marguerite.

"Papa," said Celia succinctly. "Because of Papa."

The other two stared at her. "You know it would have been so, Marguerite," she insisted. "Papa didn't approve of the aristocracy or of wealth. And Mama loved him."

Her sister nodded slowly. "You are right, I think, Celia. But then why would she have been going to see Lady Norwood—and why was she killed?"

There appeared to be no immediate answer for that, and they lapsed into thoughtful silence. Sir Richard drove them home in the chaise, and Marguerite inquired curiously why he had not gone in pursuit of Philippe.

"Because I don't wish to catch him," said Sir Richard grimly. "After all, he is my half brother. Hopefully, he will take himself out of the country without a scandal."

He paused for a moment, then continued slowly, "And you realize that it could not have been Philippe who was involved in the earlier murders?"

Marguerite nodded and Celia looked more shocked than ever. "It was Lady Norwood," said Marguerite briefly.

"I would prefer that you not call her by that name, Marguerite. That was my mother's name as well," he replied grimly.

Neither of them seemed to note that he was now calling her by her Christian name, or that she patted his hand, almost absently. "Of course. It must be terrible for you. What will we do about—my godmother?"

"I shall have to confront her with it, and then I will try to think of the least scandalous way to send her away to some quiet place to live out the rest of her days. I shall most certainly not allow her to peacock about as she has been, using my father's name."

The ride back to the Royal Crescent was quiet after that, all of the members of the group absorbed in their own thoughts. Relieved that Sir Richard no longer appeared a villain, Marguerite was ashamed to think that she had believed even for a moment that he was capable of the murder of his father. It appeared that she had misjudged him from the beginning, and she reluctantly admitted to herself that he was all that she had hoped for in a husband for Celia: wealthy, protective, handsome. He was even a very intelligent man with interests beyond those of the horse and the bottle. It seemed curious that the thought brought her so little pleasure.

Seventeen

Marguerite was determined to confront Lady Norwood as soon as they returned home, but as they entered, Stephens informed them that Mr. Alexander Clive had been awaiting their return for two hours.

"He is in the drawing room, Miss Standish," he informed her stiffly, clearly displeased by this fact. "I explained to him that I did not expect your return for some time, but he insisted upon remaining here until he could speak with you. Since Lady Norwood is still confined to her own chamber, I felt that I could take the liberty of having the gentleman wait for you there."

"Thank you, Stephens," replied Marguerite, who was also unsettled by Mr. Clive's presence. She had wished to go directly to Lady Norwood, but now she would be forced to postpone doing so. More than that, however, she did not like the effect that his earlier visit had had on Celia. Her sister had shown far too great a preference for him and for life in Northaven.

"What do you suppose has brought him such a long distance, Marguerite?" asked her sister in amazement, her eyes shining at the prospect of seeing him again. "And so soon after his other visit, too."

"I have no idea, Celia," she responded briskly, "but we shall soon know."

She paused for a moment as Sir Richard addressed

Stephens. "Has Mr. Norwood returned yet?" he asked the butler.

"No, Sir Richard. I have not seen him since he left with the ladies for their drive," replied the butler.

The sisters entered the drawing room together, and Sir Richard, apparently regarding himself as a chaperone in the absence of his stepmother, came in quietly behind them and stood in the corner of the room, watching the scene.

Young Mr. Clive stood up abruptly, and then adjusted his spectacles carefully. "I beg your pardon for intruding upon you once again," he began diffidently, as though sensing Marguerite's displeasure, but she interrupted him.

"Nonsense, Mr. Clive," she said cheerfully, extending her hand to him and hoping that he could not detect any lack of sincerity. "We are always pleased to see you."

"Is there something wrong, Mr. Clive?" asked Celia, her voice trembling slightly. "You appear distressed."

He turned to her, his dark eyes troubled. "I am afraid that I bring you bad news, ladies," he said quietly. "Mrs. Ruscombe finally lost her battle. She died last Monday afternoon."

Tears welled up in Celia's eyes and rolled down her cheeks as she drew her handkerchief from her reticule and wiped her eyes. "Thank you for bringing us the news personally, Mr. Clive. It was very kind of you to come in person instead of sending us a letter," she said softly.

Although the news was not unexpected, Marguerite found that she could not accept it quickly. Despite the fact that she had loved their kindly neighbor dearly, the reality of her death seemed to have nothing to do with her. She could not even cry, which would certainly confirm Sir Richard's belief that she was a hard-hearted woman.

Annoyed with herself for even giving a thought to his opinion of her at such a time, she made an effort to focus her attention on their visitor. Looking at him more closely, she said, "There is something more, isn't there, Mr. Clive?"

He nodded. "There are actually two things more, Miss Standish, and I confess that I am not certain how to approach either one of them."

She smiled at him and indicated a nearby chair as she sat down beside her sister. "The first thing to do is to be seated, sir. I have every confidence that you will determine the best way. Celia and I both appreciate the kindness that you showed us in Northaven and in making this journey on our behalf."

He smiled automatically as he seated himself. He did not relax, however, but leaned intently toward the young ladies. "I will begin with the more troublesome matter. When I returned to Northaven after seeing you a fortnight ago, I was determined to find the locket that Lady Norwood had mentioned."

Marguerite stirred uncomfortably. She had not intended to inconvenience poor Mr. Clive more than they already had. She had a sudden vision of him fruitlessly scouring the rectory from cellar to attic.

"I regret to say that I did not find it," he continued, "but I did find something else of importance."

He paused and stared intently at Sir Richard. "I trust that you, sir, may be depended upon to act in the best interests of the young ladies since they have no older male relative to rely upon."

Mystified, Sir Richard bowed. "You may depend upon that," he said gravely. "Just what is it that I am required to do?"

"To establish their identity, sir. As I was examining Reverend Standish's desk in the study, I discovered a spring that opened a false bottom of a drawer. Within it was a letter." He withdrew a thin document from his pocket. "It was addressed to your father, ladies, but it had already been opened and I took the liberty of inspecting its contents." Here he shot a glance at Sir Richard, as though doubting the propriety of his own conduct. "It seemed to me that if it were a matter of consequence, I could act upon it immediately and not trust its contents to the post, and, if it were unimportant, I could simply send it to you by the regular post."

"And we take it that you deem the letter most important, sir, since you have delivered it by hand," observed Sir Richard.

Mr. Clive nodded. "And so, I believe, will all of you. It is from your father, Sir Richard."

Sir Richard, taken completely by surprise, studied Mr. Clive for a moment and then silently drew a chair close to him and seated himself.

Certain now that he had their serious attention, Mr. Clive continued his tale. "This letter," he said, handing it to Sir Richard, "states that Sir Richard Norwood had discovered that his wife was an impostor. She was not Marguerite de Valencia. She was that lady's companion and her real name was Angelique D'Arcy."

There was another startled silence as they stared at one another. "Just as we suspected," murmured Sir Richard, closely inspecting the letter. "And this is my father's hand, I am certain." He handed it quietly to Marguerite, who held it as she and Celia read it together.

"As you see, ladies, this was written after your mother's death. Sir Richard—that is, the late Sir Richard," he added, glancing apologetically at the son, "wanted your father to know his wife's true identity, and to offer his own apology for the fact that Lady Norwood had not informed him of the truth immediately after your mother's death. He also promised to return any items in Lady Norwood's possession that might have belonged to Marguerite de Valencia."

Sir Richard, looking at the date of the letter, added grimly, "But he died before he could keep that promise."

They sat silently for a moment; then Sir Richard rose abruptly. "I believe that it is time that we speak with my stepmother," he announced. "It appears that she has a great deal to answer for."

Mr. Clive rose also. "Forgive me, Sir Richard, but there is one more matter that I need to share with the young ladies."

Sir Richard bowed apologetically. "Of course," he murmured, reseating himself. "Forgive me for rushing you."

"I also bear a letter from Mrs. Ruscombe to Miss Standish," he said, drawing a second epistle from his jacket.

Once again there was a shocked silence. Mesmerized, Marguerite held out her hand for the letter. It seemed impossible that she might be hearing from her dear friend who was now several days dead.

"It was, naturally, written before her stroke last autumn, and it was left in the care of her man of business, to be delivered to you in the event of her death."

With trembling hands Marguerite broke the seal and unfolded the letter, blinking back tears as she recognized Mrs. Ruscombe's familiar spikey script. When she had finished, she refolded it carefully and handed it to Celia.

"She has left me her home and her income, with the understanding that I will care for Celia and that her own servants will retain their positions." She stared at her sister for a moment and then smiled tremulously. "Thanks to Mrs. Ruscombe, Celia, we can indeed set up housekeeping together. If you wish it, we may even return to Northaven."

Celia put her arms around her sister. "You know that you have no wish to do so, Marguerite. We need not return, except to carry out Mrs. Ruscombe's wishes."

Sir Richard felt curiously empty as he watched the little scene. It was nothing to him, of course, whether the sisters stayed or went. At least they would no longer present a problem for him—they were provided for and the gentle Celia would no longer feel pressed to marry some eligible gentleman. Marguerite, of course, was free to marry whom she pleased or to take up teaching or to discover what she could about the de Valencia family. She could, in short, do anything at all—she had become a woman of independent means. Sir Richard discovered that he found this an unsettling thought. He far preferred the feeling that she was dependent upon him for her daily living.

Without ceremony, he stood and announced, "I think it would be as well to see Lady Norwood now."

Marguerite and Celia rose to accompany him, and Marguerite again extended her hand to the young clergyman, who had been watching her gravely. "Forgive us for having to leave so abruptly. I do thank you, Mr. Clive, for your kindness to me and to my sister."

Then, taking advantage of the fact that Lady Norwood was still confined to her bed, she added, "Please join us for dinner this evening, sir. We would like to talk with you when there is more time. Will you be able to come?"

"I certainly will, Miss Standish. I shall look forward to it." Mr. Clive cleared his throat nervously. "Miss Standish, might I speak with you privately for just a moment?"

Marguerite looked up, surprised by his request and the nervousness of his tone. Then she smiled pleasantly and nodded. "Of course you may, Mr. Clive." Turning to Sir Richard and Celia, she added, "I will join you very shortly in the study."

Sir Richard and Celia exchanged a glance; then Sir Richard closed the door quietly behind them. He had dismissed the young clergyman from his mind after his first visit, for it had not seemed to him that Mr. Clive was particularly worthy of the interest of either of the Standish sisters. It was quite clear both that he had been incorrect in that observation and that he had underestimated Mr. Clive.

The letter from Sir Richard's father to the Reverend Standish had provided the additional evidence he needed of his stepmother's underhanded dealings. He had always been positive that she and Philippe had been responsible for his father's death, but he had been less certain of their motive. Now he knew.

In the drawing room, Mr. Clive was looking earnestly at Marguerite. "Miss Standish, I know that you have taken excellent care of Miss Celia, and I have no doubt that you will use your inheritance from Mrs. Ruscombe to continue to care for her."

Marguerite merely nodded, not wishing to interrupt him.

"What I am requesting, Miss Standish, is your permission to ask Miss Celia to marry me. I wish that I had spoken to you before Mrs. Ruscombe's death and before I found the letter from Sir Richard's father, for I have no desire for wealth or position. I am no fortune hunter. I know that I am far from a wealthy man," he added, rushing on before she could speak, "but I assure you that I love her, Miss Standish, and that I would take excellent care of her."

"I am certain that you would, Mr. Clive," responded Marguerite. "And I acquit you of any suspicion of being interested in Celia for the sake of money or position. You were too kind to us when no profit was involved for me to think otherwise. If I am reluctant to grant my permission, it is not because you are not a man of many excellent qualities—it is simply because I want her to be happy."

"I understand, Miss Standish," he said eagerly, "but I believe that she would be happy in the life I would make for her. Celia is happiest, you know, when she is helping others, and she is truly fond of Northaven and of the rectory that was your home for so many years."

Marguerite could not deny the truth of his words, either to him or to herself. Reluctantly she nodded her head. "You may speak to her, Mr. Clive—but promise me that if she cannot say yes that you will leave her in peace."

"Agreed," exclaimed Mr. Clive fervently, again straightening his spectacles. "I shall speak to her this evening."

He bid her good afternoon and made his departure happily, leaving her with a pounding headache. It was altogether too much to deal with in one day: Tolliver had been murdered, Philippe had attempted to poison them, their mother was not Angelique D'Arcy but Marguerite de Valencia—and thus she and Celia were members of the French nobility—Lady Norwood had deceived them, Mrs. Ruscombe had died and in doing so had made Marguerite an independent woman, and Mr. Clive wished to marry Celia. Sinking to the sofa, she pressed her fingers to her temples and closed her eyes. Perhaps if she closed out the rest of the world for a bit, she would return to it to discover that all of this had been a dream.

It was only a few moments later when she found that this was not to be. Someone shook her gently by the shoulder, and she could hear a voice in the distance, saying, "Marguerite, are you quite well? What has happened to you?"

When her eyelids fluttered open, she was looking up into Celia's eyes. "Are you well, Marguerite?" she repeated. "What happened?"

"Of course I am well, Celia," she responded with characteristic briskness. "I am merely tired."

"Where is Mr. Clive?" asked her sister, glancing about the drawing room. "Has he already left?"

When Marguerite nodded, Celia's bright expression dimmed. "I see," she responded. "Did he not wish to see me?" Her disappointment was clear.

"Yes, of course he did, dear," replied Marguerite, unable to lie about it, even though she wished to do so. "He will be back a little later today."

Celia smiled and squeezed her hand. "He is quite wonderful, don't you think, Marguerite?"

"Naturally," Marguerite replied, unable to keep from smiling back at her. "And it was more than kind of him to bring us the letters. He is a remarkable young man."

Celia correctly interpreted this remark as permission to think of Mr. Clive as she chose and went happily to her chamber to prepare herself for his return. Marguerite, sighing heavily, forced herself to rise from the sofa and join Sir Richard in the study. It was of no use to try to hide. There was more to be faced today.

As she and Sir Richard made their way up the stairs to Lady Norwood's chamber, she tried to sort her thoughts. It was inconceivable to her that she was now a woman of independent means. She no longer had to depend upon Lady Norwood or Sir Richard or anyone else to care for herself and for Celia. Silently, she blessed Mrs. Ruscombe's memory.

At the top of the stairs she suddenly became aware that Sir Richard was watching her, and that he had spoken to her twice before she realized that he was speaking.

"I would like to offer you my congratulations, Miss Standish," he said gravely. "I realize that you now have other matters on your mind, but I hope that you will feel that you may remain our guests for as long as you wish."

"Why thank you, Sir Richard," she said in surprise. "I would have thought that you would be eager to see us on our way."

He shrugged. "Why? You have been no problem to me. Or, at least, only a slight problem," he amended, smiling a little. "On the contrary, I have enjoyed your contributions to our small circle. In fact, Miss Standish, I confess that I shall miss you both."

She knew, however, that although he spoke of missing them, he was a very self-sufficient gentleman, and required virtually nothing from others, certainly nothing at all from her. Undoubtedly he would miss Celia. She tried not to think about Mr. Clive and Celia, pushing them firmly from her thoughts. Although Celia liked the young clergyman, she would surely compare him to Miles Randall—or even to Sir Richard—and decide upon someone who could offer her a secure, pleasant life.

Marguerite sighed and reluctantly followed Sir Richard

down the passage to Lady Norwood's bedchamber. It was time to confront her with the truth, but Marguerite could not have been more reluctant to do so had she been the guilty culprit herself.

She had thought that she was in favor of change, that she was flexible and ready for adventure. Today she had discovered that she required more certainty in her life. The day had seen too many changes.

As this thought crossed her mind, she realized that she had focused upon Sir Richard's square shoulders as they entered Lady Norwood's chamber. No longer did he seem a threat to her. He at least was a known quantity. She knew what to expect of him. Then, remembering Mr. Clive, she sighed. What would Sir Richard think should Celia choose the young rector over him?

Eighteen

Their conversation with Lady Norwood was even stranger than Marguerite had anticipated. She was propped quietly among her pillows as they entered the room, and the maid who had been sitting with her rose silently and slipped out of the room.

"This has been a most distressing day," Lady Norwood began plaintively, her eyes closed. "I do feel that someone other than a maid should have stayed with me. Of course I suppose that I should not look for any proper show of concern from you, Richard, but I *did* think, Marguerite, that you at least would be sensible of the debt of gratitude that you owe me."

When neither of them responded, Lady Norwood opened her eyes and looked at them. One glance at their expressions caused her to sit up amongst her pillows and to straighten her cap.

"Has something else happened?" she asked, suddenly nervous. "Has anything happened to Philippe?"

"You might say so, ma'am," replied Sir Richard shortly. "Your son has attempted to poison your guests. He took them on a ride in the country and then slipped the poison into their lemonade when they stopped at an inn for refreshment. If he is at all wise, he is even now on his way out of this country to avoid charges."

Lady Norwood stared at him vacantly for a moment,

then sank back among her pillows, her face growing ashen.

"I knew that Philippe would be foolish," she murmured, plucking absently at the bedclothes. "He never uses his head. Tolliver and I told him he must be rational—"

"You told him that he must be rational, ma'am?" exclaimed Sir Richard. "And when has your own behavior been so?"

She looked at him in vague surprise. "Why, always, Richard, always. I have always done the things that needed to be done. When that foolish old woman was going to betray Marguerite and me when we first came to London, saying that Marguerite must take her rightful place in society, I knew that something must be done. And it was so easy."

She smiled up at him as though expecting him to admire her cleverness. "She took medicine for spasms, and I simply increased the dosage. No one ever suspected a thing. Our families were already dead, and there was no one to suspect or even to care about what we had done. After her death Marguerite was able to marry her parson, who despised the nobility and so would never have looked at Marguerite de Valencia, and I was able to marry your father, who would never have married a mere servant."

"Are you saying that my mother knew about the murder of her cousin?" demanded Marguerite, shocked.

Lady Norwood shook her head almost dreamily. "Of course not. Marguerite could never have understood that it was the proper thing to do. She always lived too much by the rules. How could she have ever faced her parson? Had we waited for *her* to take care of the problem, we would have waited far too long. Instead, Tolliver and I solved it. And then I was free to marry Sir Richard and live the kind of life I had always wished for."

"And free to kill him at last!" added his son bitterly.

"Well, it was necessary, Richard, but it was nothing that

I wanted to do," returned the unrepentant widow. "He had always been distressed by his estrangement from you, and then he took poor Philippe in such dislike, always holding you up to him as such a paragon."

"But how did that make his death necessary, ma'am?" demanded Sir Richard angrily.

Lady Norwood explained in the tone that one uses to speak to a fractious child. "Why, because he found the letter from Marguerite, asking me to send some of the jewels that she had left with me. She said that times had been very hard for her husband, and that she hadn't been feeling at all well herself. She wished to secure the future of her girls, in case anything should happen to her. She gave no consideration to whether or not it was a convenient thing for me to do. After all, *I* might have needed the jewels myself."

She paused and glanced up at their incredulous expressions. "Well, after all, the jewels had been *mine,* you see. I had been Marguerite de Valencia for a number of years. At any rate, Sir Richard wondered about the jewels after reading the letter—and then he told me what he thought the truth of the matter was. And he was quite right, of course—I am not Marguerite de Valencia."

She stared at them helplessly. "So you see, I had no choice. He was going to make my identity public. How could I have explained that to Philippe? And how could *I* have lived with the humiliation? Both of them—Richard and Marguerite—were causing problems for me. We had to act."

Her voice faltered, and she looked away from them. "It was so very difficult to do, however. I really dreaded losing them. I could not have done it were it not for Tolliver."

Here she stopped again, and the tears slipped down her cheeks. "If only dear Marguerite could have left the matter alone, I would not have had to—" She held out her hands to them beseechingly. "I loved Richard, and Marguerite was my dearest friend. It was tragic to lose them both in such a manner. And now poor Tolliver . . ."

The tears increased and she began to sob. "I am much to be pitied, much to be pitied," she repeated, turning her face into the pillows.

Astounded by her reaction, Marguerite and Sir Richard left the room together, Marguerite pausing to call Betsy back in to give Lady Norwood another sleeping draught and to sit with her. It was clear that she was unbalanced, and Marguerite wondered that she had not been able to detect that earlier.

"Do you think that she poisoned Tolliver?" Marguerite asked Sir Richard after they had left the room.

He shook his head. "I believe it was Philippe. I think that Tolliver was growing nervous, feeling that they had disposed of too many people. Philippe thought that she was about to give them away, for she understood what the locket meant. They had to rid themselves of you and Celia."

Sir Richard stopped at the foot of the stairs and turned to Marguerite. "I am going to see what I can discover about Philippe," he said. "I want to be certain that he is indeed on his way out of the country, and not lingering anywhere in the vicinity."

He paused and looked down at her. "I don't wish to leave you and Celia alone, however. I think that all would be well, but I wish to be certain of your safety."

"You may be certain of it, Sir Richard," said a quiet voice behind them, and they turned to see Mr. Clive and Celia standing in the doorway of the drawing room. "I would be happy to remain here until your return."

Marguerite looked at her sister's glowing face and knew immediately that Mr. Clive had made his proposal and had been accepted. For a moment she was sharply aware of the fact that their lives were about to change forever, but she was able to suppress the pang of pain and embrace Celia with a smile.

"I wish you all happiness," she whispered, and turned to extend her hand to Mr. Clive, who took it shyly.

Sir Richard, who had been looking on in astonishment, added his congratulations to the happy couple. "And I know that I may safely leave Marguerite and Celia in your care, Clive," he added sincerely, for the young clergyman had gained his genuine respect. Marguerite, fearful that he was distressed by Celia's engagement to someone other than himself, could not decide whether his manner was that of a rejected suitor putting a brave face on the matter, or whether it was that of an interested friend whose heart had not truly been engaged.

Before he could say more, they were startled by a familiar voice. "I will not ask what is taking place, Norwood," said Lord Saybrook crisply, "for it appears that we must all felicitate Miss Celia and Mr. Clive. Stephens was most reluctant to admit us and insisted upon confining us in that confounded tiny study. I see that he had his reasons, however. We apologize, Miss Celia, for forcing ourselves upon you at such a tender moment."

Miles Randall and Mr. Tavistock were following in his wake, and all three gentlemen proffered their best wishes to the happy couple.

"You did that very handsomely, Miles," said Lord Saybrook in an admiring tone. "Even I, who know better, would say that you feel no distress in this matter of the heart."

Miles and Celia both blushed, and Mr. Clive looked from one of them to the other while Lord Saybrook continued. "I have waited for someone to capture Miles for these several years. He has gone blithely on his way, leaving a trail of broken hearts behind him."

There was a murmur of reproach from Mr. Randall, but Lord Saybrook disregarded his protests and those of the others and continued. "It is only just, Miles, that at last you know what it means to be unfortunate in love. If I thought for a moment that the wound was irreparable, I would not be holding it up for inspection. Miss Celia has been the innocent cause of it, but she has done you a great kindness, Miles, for now you know that there are indeed young ladies who can engage your affections."

Here he smiled upon Mr. Clive and Celia, and again shook hands with the rector and congratulated him upon his excellent taste. Poor Mr. Clive, being unaccustomed to Lord Saybrook, was looking a little shaken, but he rose to the occasion manfully and was even able to exchange a few words with Miles.

Finally Saybrook held his glass to his eye and turned to Sir Richard. "Now, Norwood, since we all feel an interest in the well-being of your guests, perhaps you could explain to us why you are worried about their safety."

Sir Richard looked as though he would prefer to say nothing at all about the matter, and Lord Saybrook regarded him with tolerant amusement. "Now there is no point in pokering up, Norwood—although I must say that I know of no one who can do so as well as you. I have not the slightest intention of stirring until you tell me. You will recall that I have been interested in the safety of the young ladies for quite some time, and I believe that now you can tell me why they have suffered so many mishaps."

Since it was clear that Lord Saybrook meant precisely what he said and that he would not stir until receiving an explanation, Sir Richard finally gave way and explained the situation to him and his companions. They listened with gratifying raptness.

"I see, Miss Standish, that I must review my French," he said lightly, turning to Marguerite and bowing when Sir Richard had finished. "I shall look forward to the end of hostilities between England and France with even greater anticipation."

Turning to Mr. Clive, Lord Saybrook bowed and said, "I trust, sir, that you will allow us to offer our services. While I suspect that Norwood is correct and that Philippe is well on his way to foreign shores, I would be happier if the young ladies were kept very secure until we are certain of it."

He shuddered for a moment. "Poisoned lemonade! The boy must surely be mad!"

Sir Richard soon departed in search of Philippe, and the four remaining gentlemen agreed upon their assigned posts and left Marguerite and Celia in the privacy of the drawing room. Instructing Stephens to admit no one, they all settled in to wait.

Nineteen

The rest of the afternoon and evening seemed endless to the two young women. As long as they remained in the drawing room, they could catch an occasional glimpse of Mr. Clive as he paced back and forth on the green across the street, pausing occasionally to survey the area carefully. Miles Randall and Mr. Tavistock had also received their assignments: Miles was to watch the gambling house that Philippe favored and Mr. Tavistock was to watch the stable where he kept his curricle. Lord Saybrook had taken up his patrol within the house, and the servants, who had not been included in the plans, were kept in a state of upheaval by his sudden, unexplained appearances in portions of the household where guests were not normally found. The cook sent up word that she could not be expected to produce a dinner worth sitting down to if he kept popping into the kitchen unannounced and wrenching open the cupboards as though he expected to find a thief within them. The kitchen-maid, she reported grimly, was now becoming hysterical each time Lord Saybrook appeared. Stephens, whose dignity was wounded because he had not been included in the mystery, made everyone ill at ease by his manner, which was even haughtier than usual.

After sharing with Lord Saybrook the meager dinner that the cook had grudgingly assembled for them, the young ladies had gone upstairs to check on Lady Norwood. She was tossing restlessly in her bed, and Betsy was twisting her hands nervously.

"She has been acting very strange since she woke up a few minutes ago, miss," she said to Marguerite. "I have been hard-pressed to keep her in bed."

"Then she needs another sleeping draught," replied Marguerite decisively. "Give it to her now, Betsy, and after you are sure she is asleep, you may get some rest yourself. You look exhausted."

"Thank you, miss," said the maid gratefully.

There was a subdued groan from the bed, and Celia went immediately to take Lady Norwood's hand and to murmur to her soothingly. Turning back to her sister, she said in a low voice, "I think that I should stay with her, Marguerite. She has had a terrible day."

"So have you, Celia," responded Marguerite sharply. "And you are coming with me. Betsy will be able to take care of everything."

Reluctantly Celia allowed herself to be led from the chamber, and Lady Norwood's gaze followed her balefully.

Seated together in Celia's tiny bedchamber, Celia and Marguerite puzzled over the mysterious woman who had been their mother. As the evening slipped by, punctuated only by Lord Saybrook's occasional appearances, they combed carefully through memories of their childhood, trying to piece together bits of information that might give them a clearer idea of their family background, recalling every reference their mother had made to her own childhood. There had not been many.

"If Lady Norwood were well, we might be able to learn at least a little more from her," sighed Celia, who had not been able to accept the fact that their hostess was responsible for a number of deaths, including that of their own mother. "I wonder what Mama was like when she was a girl."

"Very much like you, dear child," said Lady Norwood,

gliding into the room and closing the door softly behind her. "She was greatly attached to animals, too. She had several dogs and cats and a monkey—and an aviary instead of just one bird in a cage." Here she cast a disparaging glance at Nipper, whom she detested. "And of course a great many horses. She was an excellent rider. And she was rather quiet, but very kind. The servants all adored her. Not that such things matter, of course."

She drew a chair between the girls and reached over to pat Celia's hand as though it were the most natural thing imaginable that she had dropped in to talk with them.

"Coming in to sit with me after Tolliver's death was just the kind of thing that she would have done," she continued. "Of course your mother would have *stayed* with me the entire time instead of abandoning me to the servants," she added, smiling gently.

"Lady Norwood, we thought that you were sleeping!" protested Celia, blanching at her own thoughtlessness. "Had I realized you were lying awake, I would have come in immediately."

"And you *should* be sleeping," said Marguerite, her indignation rising. Lady Norwood was acting as though nothing at all had happened—as though she hadn't admitted to three murders. And to be criticizing Celia, of all people! "Betsy gave you the potion to help you and came in to tell us that you were sleeping quietly. Why didn't it continue to work?"

Lady Norwood shrugged and her tone grew plaintive. "Who knows? Now that Tolliver isn't here to take care of me, I matter to no one. The maid probably gave me too little."

"You didn't take it, did you?" asked Marguerite sharply, watching her closely. "You must have poured it out."

"Oh, Lady Norwood, you shouldn't have done so!" exclaimed Celia in distress. "You've had a dreadful day and you need your rest."

"But what I need more than sleep is to talk to the two of you," she responded, smoothing her flaxen hair over the shoulders of her dressing gown. "I want to show you something."

Lady Norwood turned and went back to the small table beside the door and picked up an ornately chased silver box. Marguerite had noticed her pause as she entered the chamber earlier, but she had not seen her place the box there.

Returning to her chair, Lady Norwood placed the box in her lap and opened the lid. The sisters gasped. It was like opening a pirate's treasure chest—the bright jewels in their settings of gold and silver caught fire in the candlelight.

"Have you ever seen anything so wonderful?" asked Lady Norwood proudly.

Celia nodded, her eyes shining. "Yes, I have," she replied simply. "The locket that you are wearing."

Lady Norwood looked at her in surprise, then smiled—a slow, catlike smile that Marguerite found most distasteful. "Then you may have it, dear child," said Lady Norwood, unfastening the locket and placing it around Celia's throat.

Celia patted it gently. "Thank you, Lady Norwood."

"But of course."

Marguerite could scarcely control herself. The locket was not Lady Norwood's to give—it already belonged to them. Yet here she was, playing the part of Lady Bountiful. And why *was* she here? Why the desire to talk to them? Marguerite forced herself to be patient and to remain calm. Surely her reason would become clear in time. And perhaps Lord Saybrook would come to check on them shortly.

"I wanted you to see these," Lady Norwood explained, closing the lid on the twinkling rainbow of colors, "for now I think you can understand how difficult it was to consider sending any of these to your mother. She didn't ask for all of them—just for some of the pieces so that the two of you would be taken care of should anything happen to her—but how could I choose only a few? They belong together—and it was my duty to see to it that they stayed together. I was taking care of the de Valencia jewels—I am a good steward, as you see," she added, looking at the two of them proudly.

Marguerite stared at her in disbelief. "But you are not a de Valencia, Lady Norwood," she said sharply. "And these are apparently de Valencia jewels—so they *all* belonged to our mother."

Lady Norwood's pale complexion grew flushed, and her eyes brightened. "I am sorry to see that you are so mercenary—I would have thought better of my namesake."

"I'm not certain which outrageous error to correct first," returned Marguerite hotly. "How could you possibly accuse anyone else of being mercenary, when you clearly are so greedy yourself? You have committed murder for jewels, money, land, power—why you have even stolen your very name. I am most certainly not *your* namesake, but my mother's."

Lady Norwood stood up abruptly, clutching the box tightly in her hands. Her face was scarlet as she turned to Celia. "I can see that there is no point in addressing your sister. She is far too common and outspoken in manner to appreciate any fineness of feeling."

"What fineness of feeling do you possess, Lady Norwood?" demanded Marguerite. "The ability to take what is not your own, or to defend the act of murder as though it were an acceptable course of action?"

Lady Norwood looked at her disdainfully. "You are so naive, Marguerite. It would almost be amusing, if it weren't so annoying. You certainly have no imagination yourself."

Turning back to Celia, she took the girl's hand and spoke in a softer voice. "When I saw you, Celia, I truly wanted to help you for the sake of your mother. You must believe me."

Celia nodded doubtfully and her sister exploded again.

"And so you decided to help her by placing your diamond bracelet on her dressing table and accusing her of theft!"

Lady Norwood shook her head indignantly. "Tolliver did that!" she exclaimed. "I had no part in that."

"But you were responsible for what happened the next day, weren't you?" Marguerite demanded. "You gave us the list of errands and made arrangements with that man in Jarrod's for the clerk to place the card of lace in Celia's package and then accuse her of theft!"

Lady Norwood looked pained. "But of course I had to take action. You were becoming a problem, you see. Tolliver's behavior made that quite clear. I was fearful that you would grow even more suspicious, should Tolliver do anything else. You had to be gotten rid of."

Celia stared at her, horrified. "Do you mean that you would have stood by and seen me sent to jail or transported for something that I hadn't done?"

"Well, it would have solved my problem very neatly," she replied, her tone that which a practical adult would use with an unreasonable child.

"I think, Lady Norwood, that we should take you back to your chamber so that you can rest," interjected Marguerite uneasily, troubled by the peculiar light in her eyes.

Lady Norwood seemed not to hear her, however, and continued to speak to Celia. "You know, my dear, how it pains me to do this, but you must see that you have left me no choice. I must take care of my son, you know. That is my first obligation."

"What do you mean, Lady Norwood?" asked Celia, puzzled. "What are you going to do?"

"Just this," she responded with misleading gentleness. Rising suddenly and seizing a lighted candle, she moved swiftly to the curtains of the bed and set them aflame. Before the startled girls could react, she had reached the door and closed it with a snap. To their dismay, they heard her locking it from the other side.

Having regained their wits, Marguerite and Celia each reacted in a characteristic manner: Marguerite tried to pull down the bedhangings so that she could smother the flames and Celia rushed to Nipper's cage to remove him from harm's way.

"Go to the door and beat on it with your fists and call out as loudly as you can," commanded Marguerite. "Even if all of the servants are asleep, surely Saybrook will hear you!"

Celia flew to obey her, but paused when she reached the door.

"What is it, Celia? Why aren't you calling for help?" cried Marguerite, seeing that she had pressed her ear to the door. She had managed to pull down one of the bed curtains, but the covers had ignited with a frightening swiftness. She knew that she could not stop the fire alone; indeed, she wasn't certain that anyone would be able to stop it if much more time passed before she had help. Celia's tiny chamber had no window.

"Someone is with her in the corridor, Marguerite! I think that it is Philippe."

Marguerite ran to the door as the flames leapt high about her. Not bothering to try to hear anything, she threw herself against it, pounding and shouting.

"Fire! Help us!"

The door suddenly jerked open, knocking Marguerite back against her sister and sending both of them to the floor, and Lady Norwood was thrust into the room. Philippe stared down at the three of them, smiling.

"This will do quite nicely—a splendid idea of yours, Mother dear. It almost makes up for the fact that you have misled me all these years." His eyes narrowed as he stared at Marguerite and Celia. "*I* should be a de Valencia—not you!"

Marguerite started to rise, protesting, "You'll never get away, Philippe! Lord Saybrook is downstairs!"

He pushed her back down with his foot, holding his mother's casket of jewels carefully under one arm. "Lord Saybrook is trussed up like a Christmas goose in a closet downstairs—and soon he will be quite as brown and crisp as one."

As he closed the door, she called out desperately, "Sir Richard and the others are looking for you, Philippe! They will find you!"

He swung the door open a crack and smiled at her. "I fear, dear Marguerite, that Sir Richard is dead—and the others will be able to do nothing without proof." He opened his jacket and held something up. "My dear father's letter to your esteemed father—about my dear mama. I think it will be safe here with you." And, as the letter fluttered to the floor, the door closed and they heard the key click in the lock.

Celia stared at Marguerite. "He killed Sir Richard? And he would kill his own mother?" she asked in disbelief. And she turned to try to console Lady Norwood in the midst of the smoke that was filling the room. "I am certain that he will be back for you," she said comfortingly.

But Lady Norwood was not to be comforted. "My jewels," she moaned. "He took my jewels."

Marguerite was still reeling from the news of Sir Richard. For a moment she tried to stave off the pain, but it was useless. Now that he was dead, she knew beyond a shadow of a doubt that he was the one man with whom she could have been happy.

She was recalled to the reality of their situation, when Celia began to choke in the thickening smoke. Marguerite again threw herself against the door.

"Fire! Fire!" she screamed. "Help us!" As she pounded on the door once more, she heard the key rattle in the lock. Seizing the letter that Philippe had dropped on the floor, she ran it carefully under the door, lining it up with the keyhole and keeping the edge of it where she could pull it back into the room.

Jumping up, she stumbled choking through the pall of smoke to Celia's dressing table, fumbling about until she found the inevitable pincushion. Seizing it, she crawled back, hoping to avoid the worst of the smoke. Taking the longest pin she could find in the cushion, she threaded it into the keyhole and poked at the key, hoping to knock it from its place and onto the paper below. She could soon tell, however, that it was not strong enough to move the key.

Celia pulled out a hairpin, sending her hair tumbling over her shoulders. "Here, Marguerite, try this," she said, tears caused by the smoke fumes streaming down her cheeks.

She watched with bated breath as Marguerite tried again. This time they heard a satisfying *clunk* as the key hit the floor.

"If only it is on the paper," murmured Marguerite, allowing herself to breathe again as she eased the letter slowly back into the room "Please, dear God, let it be on the paper."

And the key was there, in all of its brassy brightness, and she unlocked the door quickly, helping the other two into the corridor and shutting it firmly behind them.

"Take Lady Norwood outside!" she commanded Celia. "And then send Mr. Clive to wake up one of the neighbors to send for the brigade."

"Where are you going, Marguerite?" asked Celia as she helped Lady Norwood to her feet.

"Upstairs to awaken the servants—and then I must find Lord Saybrook!" she called as she raced toward the stairs.

In a very few minutes the household was assembled on the pavement outside their home, and buckets of water were being passed up the stairs to the fire. Mr. Clive, after making certain that Celia and Marguerite were taken care of, had organized the efforts to contain the fire. The neighbors had all been awakened. Those closest to them were taking what precautions they could to protect their own property, but they had hopes of containing the fire within Lady Norwood's home.

Lord Saybrook, his vanity severely damaged by his failure to head off Philippe, apologized profusely to Celia and Marguerite. "I don't understand it at all," he said. "I don't know how he got into the house, but suddenly he was behind me and before I knew it, I was gagged and bound and locked into a particularly vile-smelling cupboard." He dusted his clothes carefully. "I shall probably reek of vinegar for weeks!"

"Lord Saybrook," began Marguerite, gathering her strength to broach the matter that she dreaded, "Philippe told us that he had killed Sir Richard."

Saybrook looked at her incredulously. "If he did so, dear lady, he did it by ambush." His face darkened. "Which, of course, is precisely the way he *would* do it. The fellow has no sense of honor."

Marguerite could find little comfort in his pronouncement. She, too, felt that Philippe would gain his ends by any means. And if he killed Sir Richard and escaped punishment, he would inherit his title, his lands, and his wealth. She sank down suddenly upon the pavement and put her face in her hands. It was altogether too much to bear. Richard was dead, Celia was about to marry, her world had shattered about her.

Lord Saybrook helped her to her feet. Although he misunderstood the reasons for her despair, thinking that her experience in the fire had unnerved her, he nevertheless took charge of the situation. Soon she and Celia found themselves installed in a comfortable room at the White Horse, and Saybrook promised them grimly that this time they would be quite secure. Three of his men were guarding their room, and Lady Norwood had been placed in a room at some distance from them, also with a guard.

Long after Celia was asleep that night, Marguerite stood at the window and stared out at the darkness. Richard Norwood was dead. It was the dark night of the soul for her. Perhaps if she had judged him differently—more accurately—she would not now be mourning his death. And the greatest hurt was that she had no right to mourn for him. She was nothing more than a temporary part of his life. She had been nothing to him.

When she finally lay beside Celia, she pictured her future: she would visit Celia and Mr. Clive at the rectory from time to time, enjoying their stories, their children, the world they had made for themselves. Thanks to Mrs. Ruscombe, she would be free to travel and to do as she pleased, but there would be nowhere for her to call home. Even Celia, who was dearer to her than life itself, would be absorbed in a world in which she had no part. Marguerite's loneliness swallowed her so completely that even the dawn brought her no relief.

She went downstairs at first light, ignoring the startled gaze of the men outside her door and those taking their breakfast in the coffee room. She was beyond caring whether her behavior was appropriate for a gently bred female. She asked the wide-eyed serving maid for a mug of coffee and retired to a far corner of the room, red-eyed and frowsy-haired and oblivious to stares.

When she heard footsteps, heavy and distinctly masculine, approaching, she prepared herself to deal with the situation. She had, after all, invited it by being a lone female in a masculine domain.

"May I join you?" The words were innocuous enough, but the voice—the voice belonged to Sir Richard Norwood. Her eyes flew to his face, quite as ravaged as her own, and then to the sling in which his right arm rested.

"I thought you were dead," she said in disbelief, still staring at him.

"News from Philippe, no doubt," he responded dryly.

"I fear he was overly optimistic—although he did give the matter his best effort. Took me quite by surprise."

"Ambushed you, do you mean?" she asked.

"I suppose you could say so. Philippe has always favored the path that offers the least danger."

"Attacked you from behind?" she probed, trying to be as casual as he.

Sir Richard nodded. "And he did a nice job of it. If his timing had been just a little better, his optimism would have been justified."

Marguerite shuddered. He was alive—standing before her alive and more or less intact—but nonetheless not interested in her. She closed her eyes and made an effort to equal his aplomb.

"I am relieved, then, that his timing was faulty," she responded coolly, her fingers gripping the coffee mug more tightly.

He nodded appreciatively. "That is most kind of you. I would have thought—some weeks ago—that you would have wished him successful in his efforts."

The tears welled up in spite of her determination to keep them down, but she would not allow them to spill down her cheeks. She smiled stiffly. "Surely, Sir Richard, you know now that I appreciate the efforts that you have made for Celia and myself. We are very grateful."

Again he nodded. "Very gratifying, I'm sure, to know that you no longer wish me dead." There was a slight pause and then he added, "I am afraid, ma'am, that I am responsible for quite a bad evening for you and Celia. Had I been quicker, you would have been spared your visit from Philippe."

She shrugged. "We are quite all right, thank you—and relieved, of course, to discover that you are not dead."

Her afterthought appeared to amuse him, and a smile creased his face. "I appreciate your concern, ma'am," he responded.

"Where *is* Philippe?" she asked, suddenly realizing that she had not learned this important fact.

"Gone," he replied briefly. "With all of his mother's property that he could gain access to—doubtless to set up a gaming house of his own on the continent. Perhaps he will attempt to win the de Valencia estates through gambling."

"How do you know this?" she asked curiously.

"I—saw him off," said Sir Richard, smiling to himself as though at a pleasant memory. "I believe that it distressed him greatly to know that I was alive—and still capable of sending him on his way."

"And what will happen to Lady Norwood?" she asked.

"She has gone, too," said Sir Richard—quite absently, as though he were telling her last week's news. "Doubtless she will lead him a merry chase. She was not best pleased that Philippe had helped himself to what she considered her jewelry."

Here he paused and walked to a cupboard in the back of the room. When he returned, he set down the casket of jewelry in front of Marguerite. "I believe, ma'am, that these belong to you and your sister. I fear that my family has been very negligent in returning them to you."

Despite her efforts, the tears spilled down her cheeks, but she attempted to ignore them. "That is most kind of you, sir," she responded coolly. "Celia and I are very grateful."

"I know that this probably means little to you financially," he said absently, staring out the window as though he were speaking to someone far away. "For I know that you are a woman of independent means now, so you have no real need of wealth."

"That is true," she agreed, quite as absently, "but of course these do have some sentimental value since they belonged to our mother—so, again, Celia and I are grateful."

"Philippe knew best how to strike at me. When he had

left me for dead and returned to the Crescent to find you,
I managed to send word to Mr. Clive. I am deeply grateful
to him and to Lord Saybrook—and to your own quick wits,
my dear."

"And so you were afraid that Philippe would harm
Celia?" Marguerite prodded him, knowing full well that
there was more to the matter than that.

"Yes, of course I was," he responded frankly. "How
could I ever replace her? Where would we find anyone
as beautiful and good as she is? Why, even Saybrook is
taken with her."

Marguerite did not look at him, afraid suddenly that she
had misunderstood his words and that he did indeed love
Celia rather than her. If so, how crushing the arrival of
Mr. Clive must have been for him.

The silence stretched out until he took her hand tenderly. "How could I ever find another such as Celia to
be my sister-in-law?"

Breathing once again, Marguerite still avoided his eye.
"Has she another sister, then, sir?"

Sir Richard turned her face gently toward him. "I see
that there will be no peace for me. I love *you,* Miss Standish—heaven help me, but I do."

He bent toward her, tilting up her chin, and kissed her
tenderly. Suddenly Marguerite heard a single bird twitter-
ing in the early dawn—Nipper, no doubt, who had accompanied them to the inn—and she began to breathe again.

Sir Richard looked at her and smiled. "Will you marry
me, ma'am, so that you may torment me at your leisure?"

Marguerite smiled at last. "You may trust me to do so,
sir." And she kissed him. Somewhere in the distance, Nipper broke into a virtual concerto of warbling. As always,
the morning had brought a new beginning.

About the Author

Mona Gedney lives with her family in West Lafayette, Indiana. She is the author of six regency romances, all published by Zebra, Books and is currently working on her seventh, *A Lady of Quality,* which will be published in December 1996. Mona loves hearing from her readers and you may write to her c/o Zebra Books. Please include a self-addressed stamped envelope if you wish a response.